MW01106227

not a matter of love

not a matter of love

Beth Alvarado

Winner of the
Many Voices Project

© 2006 by Beth Alvarado
First Edition
Library of Congress Control Number: 2005932915
ISBN: 0-89823-233-3
MVP Number 108
Cover design and interior book design by Melissa Davidson
Author photograph by Barbara Cully

The publication of *Not a Matter of Love* is made possible by the generous support of
the Jerome Foundation and other contributors to New Rivers Press.

For academic permission please contact Frederick T. Courtright at 570-839-7477 or
permdude@eclipse.net. For all other permissions, contact The Copyright Clearance
Center at 978-750-8400 or info@copyright.com.

New Rivers Press is a nonprofit literary press associated with Minnesota State
University Moorhead.

Wayne Gudmundson, Director
Alan Davis, Senior Editor
Thom Tammaro, Poetry Editor
Donna Carlson, Managing Editor
  Editorial Assistant: Michelle Roers
  Graduate Assistant: Andria Tieman
  Not a Matter of Love book team: Joel Hagen, Heather Steinmann
  Editorial Interns: Jeff Armstrong, Samuel Beaudoin, Greg Boose, Rebeca
    Dassinger, Crystal Gibbins, Joel Hagen, Michelle E. Peterson, Miranda
    Quast, Stephanie Schilling, Heather Steinmann, Jered Weber
  Design Interns: Melissa Davidson, Brenda Davis, Brooke Kranzler, Christopher
    Larson, SueAnn Lutkat, Dan Swenson, Lindsay Van Hoecke
  Festival Coordinator: Heather Steinmann
  Assistant Festival Coordinator: Miranda Quast
  Web Site Intern: Lindsey Young
Deb Hval, Business Manager
Allen Sheets, Design Manager
Liz Conmy, Marketing Manager

Printed in the United States of America.

New Rivers Press
c/o MSUM
1104 7th Avenue South
Moorhead, MN 56563
www.newriverspress.com

for
Fernando,
Michael and Kathryn

Acknowledgments

Many thanks to my friends Karen Brennan, Barbara Cully, Polly Koch, and Susan Roberts for being insightful and generous readers. To Fernando, Michael, and Kathryn Alvarado for telling me stories and giving me technical advice. To my mother who gave me a cast-iron Underwood typewriter when I was twelve. To C.E. Poverman in whose workshops the earliest stories took root. To Richard Siken, Drew Burk, and Frances Sjoberg at *spork* for making beautiful issues and including my work in them.

I am grateful to New Rivers Press, the Jerome Foundation, and the McKnight Foundation for sponsoring the MVP Competition. I would like to thank Alan Davis, Donna Carlson, Heather Steinmann, Joel Hagen, Melissa Davidson, and Taaren Haak at New Rivers Press, who transformed the manuscript into a book. Finally, my gratitude goes to the judges Alan Davis, Alice Friman and, especially, Antonya Nelson, who also chose "Just Family" for inclusion in *Ploughshares*.

and I ask myself and you, which of our visions will claim us
which will we claim
how will we go on living
how will we touch, what will we know
what will we say to each other.

—Adrienne Rich, "Nights and Days"

table of contents

bastille day

Hector Henry sat in the sun on his tiny slab of a front porch and waited for the cops. Baked and baking. One hundred and fourteen degrees. Easy. It was Bastille Day—a day the family should have celebrated, his father had told him once, as their last name used to be Henri, *Ahn-ree*, French—but on this Bastille Day, as the French were breaking bread together all over Paris, Hector had come home to find a hole punched in his front door. The apartment he shared with his dad had been robbed. His stereo was gone. This created a dull ache, black and fuzzy as a tarantula, right in the middle of his forehead, between his eyes. He couldn't see past it.

Hector squinted. The sky was the color of swimming pool water. Palm fronds were flapping in the wind like the wings of some gigantic prehistoric bird. Every morning. Every afternoon. Summer or winter. It was disorienting. The tarantula grew. Sweat was dripping in his eyes. All he wanted was the cool space music could make in his forehead, as cool as the palm of his mother's hand.

His mother had hated this place, too, he knew. That was why she'd left. Not because of his accident, not because of his father's drinking, not even because of what had happened to his sister Luisa. No, those were all just

11

additional straws. She had left the state of Arizona because there were
no seasons.

By the time the cops arrived with their notebooks and smirks, Hector
Henry felt like his brain had been breaded and deep-fried. He knew the
verdict already. Just like with his sister, nothing would be done. They would
shrug. Shit happened. Twenty-year-olds got shot. Stereos were made to be
stolen. Besides, this was one lousy stereo. One lousy stereo from Price Club
and his dad's ten-year-old TV from Sears. They wrote it down, but since
the stereo was over two years old and the TV an antique, why the insurance
would barely cover a thing, they said. Rarely did. Why, Hector would be
lucky if he could buy a Walkman! The cop with the red freckles actually
laughed as he said that.

Hector cracked open a beer and followed them out to the front step. He
made sure they saw him take a swig. So what he was only eighteen? *Oh, well.*
Let them arrest him. In front of all his nosy neighbors who were hiding
behind the blind windows of their apartments, wondering. Wondering what
had happened this time.

"Shee-it," Hector said out loud, in case anyone was listening. He planted
his butt in the plastic chair and stared at the apartment across the way where
Rita lived. Whoever had stolen his stereo frequented her apartment, he was
sure of it.

The apartment complex itself made Hector feel like he couldn't breathe.
It was tall and stucco, brown shingles and iron staircases. The eucalyptus
had leaves that rattled like coins. It looked like someone had airlifted the
whole damn thing out of a TV show about L.A. and plunked it down on the
east side of Tucson where nothing even faintly resembled the desert, except,
maybe, the Palo Verde trees the city had planted in the concrete islands,
which were supposed to give newspaper hawkers, homeless beggars, and
pedestrians refuge from the four lanes of traffic that streamed by on either
side at speeds well in excess of forty-five miles an hour. That was another
thing his mother had hated about the place. Traffic. You could hear it day
and night, a noisy river punctuated by horns and screeches and sirens.

"Where the hell are they all going?" She used to plug her ears and grimace.
"It's Tucson! What the hell is there to do in Tucson?" Hector had loved it,
back then, when his mother had sworn. Or when she'd said, in response to
some observation he'd made, "No shit, Sherlock." It made him feel older, he
supposed, part of the conspiracy she seemed to have with Luisa. It made him

feel he would some day have their cool nonchalance.

Too much traffic. Plus she hated to drive. That was why she'd sent him to get the cigarettes. After all, he was fifteen. Plenty old enough to walk across eight lanes of traffic. Not like he didn't do it all the time. And Luisa was God Knows Where doing God Knows What with God Knows Who. "That Loser, I bet," his mom had said. "I'll bet she's with that loser. She'll learn." Then she tapped the long ash off her last cigarette, sighed, and gave him a few bills so that he could cross those eight lanes to the ABCO and bring back her diet Pepsi, more cigarettes and, of course, a treat for himself. "Be careful," she'd said, her penciled eyebrows flying up in alarm like she already knew he wouldn't be.

A Nutty Buddy, that's what he was eating, quickly edging a circle with the tip of his tongue so the ice cream wouldn't melt and make the cone soggy, when he stepped off the island, heard the screech of tires, felt his back go stiff with anticipation, then flew through the air like a rag doll.

Blackness. Aqua sky. Palm fronds frightening in their ferocious clatter. The face of a man who looked like some movie star except for the little globs of white spit in the corners of his mouth. Hector remembers thinking, Who the hell? And then hearing the sucking sound his lungs made as they vacuumed in air. Then, again, nothing.

Of course, they'd had to settle out of court. Hector had stepped off the curb. The car had a green arrow. Still, the dude had been speeding and so the insurance company paid Hector's hospital bills and he got some money for his suffering. Enough to buy, on his sixteenth birthday, the most bad-ass stereo anyone had ever seen. Anyone he knew. Three, count them, three disks in the disk changer, speakers the size of small filing cabinets. The bass on that baby was enough to change the rhythm of his heartbeat. And there were times, like in that song "Try Again," when he would lie down in the darkness and put a speaker on either side of his head and the girl's voice would slide right through, all smooth and slippery, like ice soothing hot skin.

Only sound could melt away the cottony dullness left behind by the accident. Only sound kept him from thinking about how he, Hector, had been hit by a car and changed forever. About how, not even a year later, Luisa had been killed. In fact, that's right, Luisa had helped him pick out the stereo. She'd wheeled him around Price Club in his wheelchair like it was the coolest thing to do on earth. She'd said the Frankenstein scars *improved* Hector's looks. No shit. Girls *loved* a scar.

But now Luisa was gone and so was the stereo. And so was his mom. She refused to stay in a town where the killer of her daughter was walking around free. His father took it hard. Jack Daniels became his best friend and savior, for instance. "Like there's a goddamn thing I can do." That's *all* he ever said. "Whadda ya want me to do? *Kill* somebody?" Hector's mother had tapped her long red fingernails in response. Click click click against the table.

Hector glared at Rita's apartment. He knew what went on there. It was like his mom had said. "This place," she'd said, standing with her suitcase on the concrete front porch, "this place," she'd swiveled her head in a circle in such a way that Hector hadn't known if she was indicating the apartments or all of Tucson, even the mountains which caught fire almost every summer, even the saguaros that had been flipping everyone off for hundreds of years. "This place is full of crackheads going nowhere fast. Buncha zombies. Get out, Hector. Get out while you still can."

Rita had been two years ahead of Hector in school but they had both dropped out at about the same time, just after his accident, and just after hers—which, nine months later, resulted in the first of her three children. Before, when Luisa was alive, Hector used to sit with the rest of them, hammered out of his head, on the sofa. The oldest of Rita's children couldn't even toddle then but his eyes used to follow the joint as it made its way around the circle; he was waiting, always waiting, for someone to pass it to him. Of course, no one ever did, but Franklin, who later became the dad of Baby Number Three, used to, occasionally, when Rita's back was turned, blow a shotgun in the kid's face. "There ya go," he'd say and then he'd look at the rest of them and grin. "Don't say I never gave ya nothin."

"That," Gina Butt-in-ski always said, snapping her gum, "is just plain wrong."

Hector agreed, but Franklin was one big dude. Anyways, hadn't Gina ever heard of a contact high? All the kid had to do was breathe.

Hector tipped back and then forwards in his plastic lawn chair, letting it drop. He studied Rita's apartment door. Could Franklin have done it? Rita might know. Lovely Rita Meta Maid, his dad always sang whenever Hector mentioned her name. And she was lovely. Hector liked, especially, the way her capris caressed the round muscles of her calves. Also, the firm globes of her butt when she bent over to pick up the baby. That girl had some definition.

Rita was surprised to see Hector at her door. One, it was nearly eleven p.m. Two, he never came over any more, not after what had happened to Luisa. And three… three… well, three slipped her mind. But there was a number three, she was sure of it. She tapped her curving nails against her lower lip. Hmmm… he'd always been cute but, now, well, he looked different. Older. More mature. She liked the shaved head. That jagged scar. Made him look kinda tough. Kinda dangerous. Kinda like he liked her.

"Franklin here?"

She tilted her head. He did like her. "Nah. Don't see Franklin much."

"Oh."

He pressed his hand to his forehead like it hurt. His eyes seemed unfocused until she opened the door wider and he could see she was standing there in her sports bra and spandex shorts. She smiled, gratified to see she had his attention. Oh! That was number three: didn't he know she wasn't dealing any more?

"Him and me broke up."

Through the door, Hector could see Gina kneeling on the ground, like a dog, thrusting her leg up into the air behind her. She looked over her shoulder at him and grinned. "God, Rita, you coulda told me someone was here." She kept thrusting her leg in the air.

Hector wasn't sure what to make of it. He looked at Rita's chest. Her nipples were hard. She was sweating.

"Wanna come in?"

He forgot about Franklin and followed her over to the couch. She picked up the remote and hit the mute button; the people on the TV were crouched on the floor, just like Gina, doing whatever this big black guy in a leotard did.

"Tae Bo," Rita smiled at him as she lit a joint and then sharply inhaled. "Looks like you could use some," she said, her breath still drawn in.

An hour later, Rita and Hector were in her bed. She was lying naked beneath him. He couldn't believe his luck. She scooped her breasts up and pointed them at him. "I hate my tits," she said.

Hector looked at her and then, with great lust, reached over and turned on her stereo.

"Man," he sighed and buried his face in her hair on the pillow beside her, "you've got a great system."

It was Kid Rock, only God knows why, a sad song that sounded like it twanged straight out of the '70s.

Franklin, for one, was not surprised to hear (from who else but Gina Butt-in-ski) that Hector and Rita had hooked up, but he was dismayed when he arrived at Rita's a day later only to find Little Juan coming out of her bedroom. Hector, at least, used to be somewhat of a ladies' man—before he got that limp, anyways, and started hiding out in his apartment—in fact, he was the only guy Franklin knew who'd actually lost his cherry while still in junior high. But Little Juan? Little Juan was this big Tohono O'odahm dude, wide as he was tall. Wore a baseball cap, backwards, 24/7, and had a skinny ponytail that flapped down his back from underneath. Not only that, but Franklin and Little Juan had been buds for-almost-fucking-ever.

"Hey, my man," Franklin said. It was cool. Why should he care who banged Rita? After all, he could understand Little Juan's point of view: when you looked like him, you didn't turn it down. Ever.

Little Juan was putting on his shoes. "I was just hooking up those new speakers…"

"Yeah. Right. Whatever." Franklin tried to shrug off his suspicions.

But later, privately, after the idea had been buzzing around in his peripheral vision, he said to Rita, "Wha'z up with you and Tonto?"

"He's sweet." She gazed up at him, coyly. She wanted Franklin back. She knew Gina was after him and who wouldn't be? He was tall, he was blond, he was cut. And—he had good weed.

"Little Juan? Sweet?"

"But you're more fun." She pursed her lips and gave him her best dirty-little-girl expression. "Jealous?" she teased, moving closer so she could rest her forearms on his shoulders. She pressed even closer, perched on one leg, and started running her foot up and down his Levis. Teasing. Just to rub it in, she called out to Gina, who was in the kitchen trying to light her cigarette off the gas stove, "Franklin's jealous."

"At least tell me you were drunk."

"Okay." She pulled his face down to hers. "I was drunk."

But when her lips touched his, he suddenly got the picture he'd been trying to avoid: first Hector and then Little Juan sweating and grunting on top of her. He pulled away. "He bang you with his hat on?"

"I didn't do shit with him. God." She let her hands drop.

He just laughed. "Right," he said. "Like I'd fuck a bitch who fucks fat

Indians."

When Franklin walked out of Rita's apartment, he was momentarily
blinded—the sun was that bright, mid-day, July—and so he couldn't tell,
at first, who belonged to the fist that hit him square in the chest. He held
his hands up, "Whoa, man…" He squinted. Hector.

"You steal my stereo?"

Franklin stepped back. "Dude."

"Three people saw you."

"Like that means shit."

Hector squinted up at Franklin. What if it was true? The old lady in 305
had just said a blond fellow. Tall. She hadn't said Franklin. He scratched the
back of his neck. He'd been so sure. All morning while he'd been lying on his
bed, thinking about Rita, wishing he had some tunes, especially Kid Rock to
remember her by, wanting music to commemorate the slow slide of his skin
on hers, while he was hearing, instead, the sound of birds, the arhythmic
chirping of birds, birds driving him crazy, it had made sense that Franklin
was the one. In fact, Hector had come to believe that Franklin had stolen the
stereo in advance, as revenge, had taken the one thing that meant something
to Hector because he knew, somehow, that Hector was going to take Rita
away from him. It had all made cosmic sense.

"Insurance ain't gonna give me dick."

"Dude. Chill."

Hector pressed his fingers to his forehead. The tarantula was back.
Franklin was walking towards his ride and Hector was being pulled along
as if by a magnet. The car was an old Porsche Franklin had been fixing
up, primer-gray right now but some day it'd be the bomb. They got in and
the engine started with a thrum. Man, what wouldn't a little *mota* money
buy? Hector started looking at his job at Home Depot in a whole new
light. Stacking those boards on top of one another day after day. All those
stupid people asking him questions and then walking away, pissed, like they
thought he was retarded.

Franklin peeled out of the parking lot. He reached over and the CD player
sucked the disk in like a tongue and the music Hector had been thirsting
for filled his head. He took the joint Franklin offered. He leaned back and
watched a sky, flat and blue as ever, slide behind the palm trees. A few
cottony clouds were stuck coming over the mountains. He closed his eyes.

Hendrix, the guitar like smooth electricity, pure and white-hot, searing its way through the midnight space that was his brain.

And then, suddenly, silence. Hector opened his eyes. Franklin's mouth was moving but Hector was still filled with the reverberations of Cross Town Traffic. Tire tracks up and down *your* back. Hector stared at him. Franklin's eyes were bloodshot as hell. Hector concentrated. "Little Juan's trying to make his move. Rita. He was hooking up speakers for her."

Hector sat up. "Huh?"

"Yeah. This morning. That's what he said." Franklin grimaced. "But, man, he was putting on his fucking shoes."

Then Franklin cranked the sound up to full blast and the guitar, like a snake, began to slither its way down, through Hector's ears, past his heart, and into his belly.

In the parking lot, Franklin reached across Hector and pushed his door open. "Not only did he rip you off, my man, but he did the nasty with Rita."

Hector just stared at Franklin's face. It was red and melting. Unnatural. Like a bad acid trip.

"Payback's a bitch," Franklin was singing, "payback's a bitch."

Hector got out of the car and left Franklin to melt in the sun. He wondered if the heat could melt those wrinkles in your brain, the ones where you kept your thoughts and memories. Maybe. He sure was having a hard time. The sun robbed everything of its moisture. That's what would happen to him. The sun could suck the moisture out of his brain through his eyeballs if he weren't careful. He closed his eyes until he could barely see through the fringe of his lashes. His mom and Luisa had always teased him about them and now, just the other night, Rita had said, "My God, look at your lashes. Hector, baby, you're beautiful." He could still feel her hot breath on his closed lids. Her breast resting on his shoulder as she leaned against him to get a better look. Her mouth against his as she breathed the smoke into him during their first kiss.

Maybe he would forgive her if she had his speakers.

Maybe not.

Up the stairs and into his father's dark apartment. He drank the soda right out of the liter bottle in the fridge. Like anyone cared, now that his mom was gone. Then he poured some salsa from the jar into the half-full carton of cottage cheese. Damn. No chips. No chips anywhere. But wasn't that always the way? You had salsa, you didn't have chips. You had chips, you didn't have salsa. It was like music and chicks. You couldn't have both at the same time. One or the other. Maybe. If you were lucky.

And he knew that as a general rule, he, Hector Henry, was not among the lucky. No, it was sorry-ass drug pushers like Franklin who always had the girl, always had the wheels, always had the tunes, always had the *dinero* and the *mota*. So who'd done it? Franklin or Little Juan? Franklin had said Little Juan. Franklin had held a wad of bills in his hand and said, why would I steal your boom box? Franklin had money up the ass. That was true. But it didn't mean he didn't want more. Rich people were like that.

Plus Franklin was jealous. Hector was sure. After all, Rita liked him now. Hadn't she rubbed her breasts against him? Kissed him first? Hadn't she let him put the speakers on either side of the bed so that when they were lying between them, naked in one another's arms, the music could move through them and synchronize their heartbeats?

Why was it guys like Franklin who always got chicks pregnant, anyways? If Hector had a kid, he would take it to the zoo. He would let it sit on his lap and eat right off his plate. He would never let anyone blow dope in its face. Not even somebody as big as Franklin.

Damn. Hector could see it now. It wasn't enough that Franklin took his stereo. He wanted to take Rita away from him, too.

Hector jabbed the spoon into the cottage cheese and salsa mixture so hard it splattered. Double damn. He wanted some chips. Some Ruffles, to be precise. With salt all along their ridges. He wanted to lick the salt off the ridges. He loved to eat chips that way. Nibble, nibble, nibble. God-dammit. He'd rather have chips than salsa. He took another swig of soda. It was flat. Wouldn't you know it! He went into his bedroom to turn on the stereo and then, it hit him again, with the full force of Bastille Day, the damn thing was *gone*.

For. Ever. Fuck.

This was going to be his life. He could see it now. This was his life story.

Timothy, the nerdy white guy who lived next door to Rita, was wearing a jaunty hat and boxer shorts when Hector showed up at his door and asked to borrow his gun.

"Sure," he said, ushering Hector into his dim apartment, "wanna beer?"

Hector nodded. He was feeling a little shaky. Maybe a beer was just what he needed.

Timothy came out of the kitchen with two cold ones by the necks in one hand and a gun in the other. The hat still perched on his head. Hector took a beer and the gun and sat on the couch.

"Whad'ya think?" Timothy asked.

Hector looked up, surprised.

"Think the ladies'll notice?"

"Sure," Hector nodded. "It's dapper."

"Dapper?" Timothy laughed.

Hector smiled. "Dapper, indeed."

Timothy looked at himself in the hall mirror. Sucked in his gut. Stuck his scrawny chest out.

Hector took several gulps of the beer. It was just the right thing on a hot day. He could see why his dad liked it so much. He put the bottle down on the coffee table and weighed the gun, first in one hand and then the other. Then he pointed it at the TV like he was aiming. It wasn't too heavy. Just right. Like the beer. Which he finished.

Timothy was still studying himself in the mirror when Hector stood up. "Thanks," he said, "for the brew and the piece."

Timothy turned and held his beer up in a toast, "Here's to both our guns hitting their targets."

But Hector was already on his way out.

When Rita answered her door, Hector halfway just wanted to forget it. He imagined her pulling him in, straight through the living room, past all the dopes on the sofa, straight into her bedroom, straight into her bed.

His eyes were ready to praise her.

"Hector," she smiled, "maybe you ought to come back later."

Franklin *and* Little Juan on the couch behind her? Gina sitting in some weird upside-down position in the armchair, eyes closed. Two kids asleep in the playpen next to Gina, the oldest, coloring on the floor. At least three other people he didn't know passing a bong. Smoke was billowing past him, out the door in big sweet clouds. Franklin told Rita to quit advertising.

Hector could hear the stereo from the bedroom, the bass was awesome. He pushed his way in. Rita was a little surprised, but if he wanted to get into it over her, oh, well. Who was she to stop him? Maybe Franklin would learn to appreciate her.

Hector pushed his way into the bedroom. They were huge speakers; they weren't his. So where were his? He could hear something inside his head snap. Next thing he knew, he was pulling Little Juan up off the couch by his tee shirt and yelling at him. If he hadn't been blinded by the color of his own anger, which was a bright yellow at that moment, he would have seen the confusion in Juan's eyes.

Juan was shaking his head. "Hey, man, what're you talkin' about?" He was befuddled not only by the unexpectedness of Hector's anger, but also by the pot he'd been smoking all afternoon.

Hector waved the gun in front of his face and then over at Franklin. "You or him?"

"Man, man, cool it, man," Juan stammered. "What're you talking about?"

Franklin held his hand out. "Chill. Dude."

His voice was so calm, it made Hector crazy. Like *he*, Hector, was the one who was full of shit. He jabbed the gun towards Franklin.

"Godammit," Rita's voice cut through, "take it into the other room."

And so they did. They went into Rita's bedroom but the sight of the rumpled bed just made it harder for Hector to think. He pointed the gun at Franklin. "You said Little Juan took it."

Juan burst out, "What the hell? Why'd you go and tell him that?"

Franklin looked at Hector and then pointed at the speakers. "How d'you think he bought those?"

"Bull! Shit!" Juan was looking at Franklin.

"Just tell him, dude. Give him the money."

Little Juan lowered his head like a bull and rammed Franklin in the chest; Franklin started pummeling his back. They weren't paying any attention to Hector at all. The sound of their voices pounded in his head. He opened his mouth and a roar came out. They both stopped. He pointed the gun at Franklin. At Franklin's leg. Pulled the trigger. But it didn't go off. He tried again. Nothing.

Click click click.

The fucking thing was fucking broken.

Useless.

Hector looked at it and shook it.

That was when Franklin started laughing. "Oh, man, Hector, you fucking had us going. Oh, man," and as Hector turned and left the apartment, all he could hear was Franklin's laughter. Franklin's laughter. Like a surgeon's saw, grating and whining its way into his skull, splinters of bone flying.

Next door, it took three knocks before Timothy answered. He was fully dressed, hat still perched on his head like he thought he was Frank-Fucking-Sinatra.

"This thing's a piece of shit," Hector said, waving the gun in front of him.

"Wha'd ya mean?" Timothy took it from him.

"It's broken. It doesn't work."

Timothy shook his head, studying the gun. "Safety's on," he said, and then he clicked it off. "And you've got to put a bullet in the chamber." He slid the mechanism and gave it back to Hector.

"Now it should work?"

"Damn straight," Timothy said, before he shut the door.

"*What*?" Rita demanded when she opened the door and saw Hector standing there with the gun in his hand.

"They still here?"

"Where else?" she rolled her eyes towards the bedroom. "And don't be so loud about it. You woke the baby."

Hector didn't say nothing. He was sorry the baby woke up but, oh well. He guessed it would go back to sleep with all that pot smoke in the air. He was suddenly mad at Rita. His mother may have left him, but she never woulda let shit like this happen in her house. If Rita was gonna stay with him, things would have to change. No more dope in front of the kids. Even if they weren't his.

Franklin and Little Juan were still going at it. They didn't notice Hector. There was a bottle of tequila open on the dresser. He took a couple of swigs and closed his eyes. The burn calmed him down. His mother, who was over half Indian and less than half Irish, had always told him and Luisa, "One drop of Indian blood and tequila'll make you crazy. One drop of Irish and it's all poison." But his father had told them the French blood canceled everything else out. Just to piss their mom off, he used to give Hector and Luisa beer from when they were little. "If you're weaned on it," he'd say, "you'll never have a problem." Hector took another swig. He figured his dad was right. Everything was becoming much clearer: Franklin had done it. One more gulp. The burn cleared his brain. Almost like music.

When Hector opened his mouth, Franklin and Juan turned so suddenly, they fell against one another. Franklin pushed Juan away and looked at Hector, laughing. Like he thought nothing could ever come around and hit *him* in the head.

Little Juan started backing away. "You know you sold it," he said to Franklin.

"Me? You'd do anything to hump Rita."

Hector watched through a red haze as Little Juan lunged at Franklin, but Franklin was just holding him out at arm's length, laughing, always laughing. "Only way you get pussy is to pay for it."

Hector was on fire. Maybe it was the tequila, maybe the picture of Juan on top of Rita, maybe the noise of Franklin's voice, how it never stopped, how it whined its way in, causing damage, causing bleeding, causing that thing in his head, that blood vessel thing the doctor had warned him about, to burst. Everything went red and pulsing. A roaring came out of his mouth.

Little Juan suddenly quit pummeling Franklin and looked straight at Hector.

Franklin, right next to him, looked like an air traffic controller: this way, this way, this way: he's your man. Bust a cap in *his* ass.

Juan stammered, "Dude, Hector, I was tight with your sister."

"How tight is tight?" Franklin started snickering. "That's what Hector wants to know."

Luisa. It was suddenly clear as water: they thought this was a joke, they thought he was a loser like his dad, they thought he'd never have the balls to use a gun.

Hector pointed in the direction of their legs and there was a sharp sound and then again, it went off, Franklin was yelling and Juan was making these noises and Hector shot again and Juan was falling and Hector shot again and Franklin shut the fuck up.

Finally.

It was quiet.

Hector turned and left. They would not fuck with him again. They would not steal his shit again. They would never laugh at him again.

Out in the living room, everyone was watching the TV. As Hector walked through the room, he expected someone to say something, but no one said a thing. Later, he heard, someone told the police they remembered a pair of turquoise sneakers. Converse, maybe.

When Hector stepped out of Rita's apartment, it was windy and the lightning had already started. He loved nights like this, lived the whole year in this shit-hole of a town just so he could see the summer storms. He decided to walk to the high school so he could climb up to the very top of the bleachers and watch lightning cross the desert. No matter what direction the storm was coming from, he'd have a good view. It used to drive his mother crazy when he and Luisa would do that. "Don't you know you're a coupla lightning rods?" she used to shout after them.

But Hector knew different people had different kinds of luck and his was that he'd never get struck by lightning. As it turned out, that was true for Luisa, too. She got shot instead. They never knew who did it. When they found her, her head was like a melon. Split open. Part of the skull, gone. The earth was so dry, it had drunk his sister's blood.

He was crossing the field towards the bleachers when he heard someone run up behind him. Franklin. But Hector didn't care. The storm was taking all the anger and confusion out of him. Wind was like that, the way it rushed over his skin. Lightning, too, it made him think about God or nature or something. About how there were things more powerful than people. About how Franklin just might have the kind of luck to get hit by lightning.

Franklin put his arm around him, "Hey, bro, where're you headed?"

Hector indicated the bleachers with a jerk of his head.

"Mind if I join you?" Franklin asked, lighting a joint and handing it to him.

Hector shrugged. "Sure you wanna risk it?"

But Franklin didn't get it. He just kept saying how Hector had showed Little Juan. How although he, Franklin, had had nothing to do with the stereo, he was still gonna be sure that Hector got his money. After all, Hector was one stand-up dude. Just like Luisa. Man, if anyone ever had balls, it was Luisa.

"I shit you not," Franklin said, "first thing tomorrow, I'll get it from Little Juan. In fact, I'll take you to get the money and then we'll go pick out a new system. You can get whatever you want."

"Sky's the limit," Hector said, climbing the bleachers. Funny how a little gun made people pay attention.

"Sky's the limit," Franklin agreed.

Once they were at the top, Franklin quit making promises. He quit talking, period. Maybe it was first time he'd ever noticed lightning.

Hector loved the way the clouds crossed the sky. Sometimes the lightning came in a sheet and illuminated everything. Sometimes it came down in a bolt and split the sky in half. Sometimes a bolt came up from the ground to meet the electricity in the sky. They met there in the middle somehow, like two long jagged fingers of light. Sometimes the air was so charged, it caught fire.

For the longest time, they sat there, leaning back, passing the joint back and forth. In a way, it made Hector sad. He realized how much he missed Luisa. Nothing, no one, would ever replace her.

When the rain came, it came in sheets. Hector and Franklin decided to hightail it, but it was slow going. The metal bleachers were treacherous, they kept sliding on them, and when the lightning flashed white as sunshine at noon, they froze in their tracks. Stop action. As if they feared they'd been chosen. As a result, they were soaked by the time they hit the ground. By then, the field was so muddy, it sucked at their shoes as they ran. They were sloshing down the sidewalk towards the apartments, when a car pulled up and some Mexican guy Franklin knew leaned out and asked them if they wanted a ride.

Franklin and Hector climbed into the back seat. The car's AC was spewing out lukewarm air that smelled like stale beer and cigarette smoke. Franklin and the driver started talking about kilos. Someone turned the stereo back up. Beastie Boys. Hector loved the Beastie Boys. He was looking out the window at the haloes of rain around the street lamps. He was shivering. He was twirling something in his fingers, trying to get warm.

And then the car stopped. The music stopped.

The driver said, "Dude, what the fuck're you doing?"

Hector looked up. The driver and the Mexican guy riding shotgun were turned all the way around, staring at him.

"What?" He looked at Franklin to see if he had a clue.

"You the dude killed Little Juan?" the Mexican asked.

Franklin was staring at Hector, too. At his hands. Then he looked at the guys in the front seat. "Little Juan's dead?" Franklin asked.

Hector looked down. His hands were twirling Timothy's gun around.

"For sure?" Franklin stammered.

The Mexican just shook his head.

"Shit," Franklin said. "Oh, shit."

25

"Get the fuck out," the driver said.

Hector was studying his hands. "I can put it away."

The Mexican laughed. "Dude's crazy."

"You killed him," Franklin said, "you killed Little Juan."

"Little Juan's dead?" Hector looked at Franklin.

"You retarded?" the driver shouted. "Get the fuck out!"

Hector raised the gun and pointed it at him. "Click," he said.

He had never seen three people get out of a car so fast in his life. They didn't even bother to take the keys or shut the doors. He laughed. But then his laughing got all weird, like crying. Could it be true that Little Juan was dead? He didn't know what to do. Should he go to Rita's? Should he throw the gun away? He reached over the seat and turned the music back up. The decision was so heavy, he just sat there, slumped over the seat. He closed his eyes. It was still the Beastie Boys, *I can't stand it, I know you planned it*, an oldie but a goodie, as his dad would say.

When the song was over, he climbed out of the car. The rain was spitting in his face. He got in the driver's seat and pretended it was his car—after all, he would probably never have one. Not at this rate. He cranked up the stereo and drove himself home.

When Hector woke up, the air was so humid and hot, he felt like he was swimming in tomato soup. The afternoon sun was blaring in across his bed and, instead of birds, he could hear the screaming of the cicadas. The faucet dripped in the bathroom loud as a tin drum. He put the pillow over his face. He wanted it to be dark and quiet, but there, in the darkness, he remembered Little Juan. He remembered the sharp popping sound of Timothy's gun. But hadn't he shot only at Juan's legs? He saw Little Juan falling. It was all so confusing. And noisy. But he was sure he had shot only at his legs. He would never have shot at his head. Not after what had happened to Luisa, her head split apart like that, like she didn't matter to anyone.

Your legs weren't who you were. Not like your face. Not like your brain. Not like your heart. He hadn't wanted to rob Little Juan of who he was. He hadn't even wanted to hurt him, really. He had just wanted the noise to stop. He had wanted his stereo back. He had wanted them to listen.

Hector wished his mother could come and sit on his bed. She would put her hand on his forehead and say, "Hmm. You're burning up, boy." Then she would go and get a wet wash cloth and wash his face and wash his neck, again and again, and his shoulders and his arms and his hands, until his fever was gone. He remembered how she had cried when Luisa was found. How she'd said she hoped it wasn't an Indian who killed her. "Enough dead Indians around," she'd said, "without us killing off each other."

But they had never found who killed Luisa. For a while, they thought it was her loser boyfriend. One cop said Luisa had killed herself. Sometimes Hector thought that was true, maybe Luisa had wanted to go back into the earth. Be one with the elements. That's why she'd let the earth suck her blood dry. Maybe the lightning that shot up from the ground was partly her. Her fire, at least.

He got up and took a shower. He dressed in his jeans and his best shirt and sat at the table for a long time, the gun in front of him. His mother would find out if he did to himself what Luisa might've done. She would find out if he had killed an Indian. He didn't know which was worse.

He stood up. His hands were shaking as he dialed 911. He didn't know why fear felt like love, why it made your heart beat so hard, even up into your throat, but it did. The blood in his ears was so loud he could hardly hear the woman; he could hardly hear himself tell the man that he had the gun.

Little Juan was dead. It was true. Later, Hector would find out that one of the bullets had pierced an artery. Juan had bled to death, there in the room all by himself. After Franklin left. While everyone else was smoking dope and watching TV on the other side of a wall as thin as cardboard. Even lovely Rita. She'd found him an hour too late, when she went in to bed.

Hector never did know how it happened, he knew only that he hadn't meant for it to happen. He felt for Little Juan's mother the same sorrow he felt for his own. He wondered if she would have to move out of town, too, far away from the place that had taken her son.

He rested his forehead against the cool wood of the table. He hoped Juan didn't have a little brother, but that was something he didn't want to think about. Instead, he concentrated on the dark place in his forehead, on letting the coolness of the wood seep in. Wood was something you could rely on, like stone. Something strong. He would be like that. Immoveable. When they came to ask him, he would not lie.

comadres
in the
kitchen

"These," Bernadette pointed to black-and-white prints Rainy had just matted. The ocotillo, like prison bars, divided the sky. Prickly pear pads, close up, were fleshy, penetrated by the thick spikes of their needles. In one, the sky was open and flat, defined by the dark edges of the mountains; it contained the curve of a single cloud. "We could hang these."

Bernadette had decided that Rainy needed a make-over—not in the looks department but in the life, the *career*, department. It was the least she could do. Just because you're middle-aged, she wanted to tell her, doesn't mean you're invisible. Doesn't mean, in the words of that Virginia Woolf character whose name she had forgotten, you are not so gifted as at one time seemed likely. Please. As if with the decline of the body came the decline of everything else: the mind, ambition, talent.

"I could see these anywhere and recognize them as yours," she told Rainy, wife of her ex-husband. How long ago that all seemed, eons, before recorded memory.

Bernadette was looking at what Rainy called the *Saguaro Series*. They were tall shadows of cacti on a hill at night, the smudged points and blurred streaks of the city lights below them. Rainy had spent over a year doing that series. She'd had to leave the house while everyone else slept. As she slipped out of bed, away from J's warm body, she'd felt an illicit thrill, almost as if she were having an affair. She'd load her cameras and tripod, extra film, into the car and head for a different hill every night. She often had to pick her way in through the cactus, the equipment digging into her shoulders and throwing her off balance, the sharp needles of the prickly pear tearing at her pant legs. During the monsoons, there were lightning flashes in the distance; once she caught a crooked finger of light as it came down and touched the earth.

On those nights, the solitude was heady. Somehow, out in nature, at night, she was Rainy. Just Rainy. Not J's wife. Not Lydia's mom. Not the boys' step-mom. She pictured herself as the "not," the circle, the empty center of a spider's web: each sticky strand represented someone in her life, some tie to the universe. On those nights she knew what it would be like to have those strands severed, to be not only alone but absent. Say, if someone were to come upon her and kill her, it could happen, or if she were to get in the car and just drive. That's what she meant by aloneness; at the moment of death, it wouldn't matter who was standing around your bed. The people in your life would be like saguaros: shadowy figures, standing guard but fading, unable to hear you.

She remembered craning her neck to watch them as they swayed ever so slightly in the wind. They were ancient beings. They had kept watch on the hillsides for hundreds of years, since the valley was mostly desert and green, no concrete, no waves of heat rising from buildings and black asphalt. They had watched the lights in the basin get brighter and stretch farther and farther with each year, with each decade. They gave her an overpowering sense of the passage of time. As she watched Bernadette look at the photographs, she knew she felt it, too: the sense of permanence, the sense of loss.

"I've been thinking," Bernadette said slowly, "that if the boys came and stayed with us on the weekends—Lydia, too, if she wanted—you could have some time to concentrate on your work. Get your career going. I mean we can hang these in the café for starters. And I've got friends, artists, in San Miguel. You know, contacts."

"I *have* a career," Rainy said. "The bookstore."

She left it at that. Bernadette would never understand that photography was her secret vice. She kept the evidence hidden in the same way an alcoholic might squirrel empty bottles under the sink. Exposure could equal pain.

Berna's hair was black with silver streaks that day. Oddly enough, Rainy thought, it looked almost natural on her. Of course, the short black dress, black stockings, and red cowboy boots were a bit much.

This is what she knew of the marriage of Bernadette to J: Berna had been one of those women who was so sure she was right, the possibility of another perspective never occurred to her. She would talk everything to death, keep J awake whole nights, knowing he would give in, finally, just to get some sleep. Berna, what a disaster that had been. If I could be happy with a man, she'd told him, it would be you. This was not good—according to J—not good. How could he have got something so fundamental as sex wrong? For months, he and Bernadette had lived a completely hedonistic life, disconnected from everyone else. He remembered patchouli oil and pot smoke, the showers they took together every night, wine and margaritas and vodka-spiked watermelon, crusty bread, steaks on the grill, peeling the shrimp out of their buttery shells. It had been hazy, like summer could be, hallucinatory in its heat. By November, she'd found herself pregnant with twins and so they had married. The twins had weighed her down, literally, of course. She had settled onto the couch and become mother earth herself. He, in the meantime, had become invisible. *Persona non grata.* An accessory after the fact.

"Really," Bernadette said, moving her finger over a print as if she were tracing the shapes in the air, "it's the least I can do."

Rainy could feel the slow burn. But it wasn't time, she didn't resent one minute spent with the boys; it was resources. After Berna inherited those beaucoup bucks from some dead relative's oil well, she'd had the luxury of sinking her money into her travels and then, the café, when the boys needed clothes, a better computer—not to mention the tons of food they consumed. Plus, Jesse could have used a tutor and Ben a college fund.

Not to mention this fact: now that she was back in town after ten years, Berna wanted to bond. She had taken the boys to *Puerto Peñasco* with her a few weeks ago and let them get shit-faced. They were seventeen. They had come home doing pantomimes about how difficult it was to walk in sand after too many pitchers. Jesse would do the running man in slo mo, making sucking sounds as he tried to lift each foot. Ben had been convinced that if you didn't believe in gravity it didn't exist.

And, swear to God, Jesse said, he walked off the end of the sea wall and took five steps in the air. Five steps! Before he fell! He was walking on air!

It can be done, Ben had insisted, there is no reason the molecules in the air can't be as solid as the molecules in a wall. They just vibrate at different frequencies.

Is this scientific theory, Rainy had asked him, laughing in spite of herself, or drunk man's theory?

But that night, images of Mexican jails kept disturbing her sleep. Dirty straw strewn on the floor for beds. Rats. The sound they would make, the scritch, scratch as they scurried across concrete.

Bernadette was worried about Jesse and this older woman he'd been dating. Nora. A skinny hairdresser with blue hair. (It made no sense that the hair color bothered her. Okay. She knew this.) A tattoo that looked like a lightning strike down the back of her bony neck. A pierced lip—who knew what else was pierced? "Berna, Berna, Berna," a little bird's voice pecked at the inside of her head, "you of all people want Jesse to find someone *conventional*? A born-again Christian maybe? A Mormon in a flowered skirt? A bank teller in career-wear from K-Mart?" No, it wasn't that. How could *she* be such a snob? She with her Oklahoma Cherokee/Irish dirt-poor Evangelical roots? It was the two little girls. Plain and simple. Jesse had taken Nora and the girls over to her house for dinner Saturday. It was the two little girls. Bernadette hadn't been prepared for them. Wasn't there something strange about a seventeen-year-old boy and a twenty-year-old woman? A twenty-year-old *mother*. Only three years, but a lifetime apart.

Jesse had sat with the girls on the big rug in the living room and built forts and towers out of blocks—the younger girl took the most delight in knocking them down, of course, which dismayed her older sister. Nora and Bernadette had sat on the couch and watched, laughing at the fact that Jesse was as intent on the game as the kids were. When Nora passed by Jesse on her way into the kitchen, she ran her fingers lightly through his hair in a gesture of intimacy and tenderness that was so natural, it made Bernadette's eyes tear. Still.

"This Nora," she said to Rainy. "I don't want him to get saddled with someone else's kids."

"Children are easy to love."

"He's seventeen."

"It's not like they're getting married next week."

Bernadette couldn't believe Rainy. What was Jesse going to do? Work as a mechanic his whole life? Some of the still-dripping prints were of Nora and the girls. Obviously Rainy knew them. She'd spent a lot of time with them. And here Bernadette had just met them. Why did that even matter? But, of course, it did. She wished, in matters of the heart, that the boys would confide in her first.

There were prints of Tammie and the little sister, Millie, blowing bubbles in the front yard, the lips round, the curve of their cheeks, the bubbles, all a study in the roundness of babies. Millie's dimpled fingers were poised as if she were plucking the strings of the guitar as Jesse played a song for her. And Jesse. A shot of his head bent over the guitar, his sandy hair falling in his eyes. Then Nora's head bent, next to his, as she listened. Lydia and Tammie, their noses touching, gazing into each other's eyes.

One afternoon. Gone. What else had she missed? Had Rainy documented every afternoon? Bernadette was sure there were pictures of the boys with chocolate frosting smeared around their mouths. In long colorful shorts on skateboards. In bathtubs, on horses, at bat. And then her own life intruded: San Miguel, the deep blue walls and cobblestone streets, the garden in the center of town. She had met Marisol there. She had sung in a few of the bars. She had painted and hung her paintings. She had learned to make *mole*, Marisol's hands guiding hers as she ground seeds in the *molinito*, as she mixed the *masa* for *tamales*. *Chili rellenos*, the firm flesh and bite of the *chili*, the smooth, rich goat's cheese. Marisol's smooth lips. Lying in bed with Marisol, the soft vowels of Spanish sighing like the sea, invading even her dreams, changing the neurons and pathways in her brain. She had created a new self. And Rainy had created, what? A home. A few photographs. She could look into Rainy's heart and see a blank slate. Rainy was still on hold.

Getting saddled with someone else's kids—who between them had *that* particular experience? Oh, Rainy would have loved to be able to say that *just so*, off-hand, a hint of sarcasm. But she'd always had a heavy hand with the pepper. There was too much truth to be flippant—deciding to marry J would have been a snap had it not been for the boys. *If anyone understands Jesse's predicament, it's me.* Would that do? As it was, she and J had taken a pre-wedding honeymoon trip to decide, left all three kids with Bernadette and took—as it turns out—their only long weekend trip to anywhere sans kids in the ten years of their marriage.

They had picked San Diego, as if the sea air would clear their heads, her head, more precisely; J already knew what he wanted. The last night, there was a storm. Rainy had come to no decision and so she had been sitting on the balcony by herself trying to imagine living in a house with three children—her four-year-old daughter and twin boys, seven—no wonder J was anxious to tie the knot! She found herself thinking of marriage as if it were a *space*, a house she might buy. Was there a view? What was the light like? Were the rooms big enough? Would there ever be any silence? The palm trees were jerking around. A few drops of rain hit her face, cold, it was cold that night; the white caps were skimming along the dark water, no line between water and sky. Then she saw a woman walk out into the surf.

She was sure she saw this: the woman, of slight build, tucked her dark hair into a little white cap; she fastened the strap under her chin and then she strode surely into the water. She dove. She looked like a dolphin breaking through the stormy waves, and then her white arms flashed, her white round head turned, as she started to swim out beyond the breakers.

Just then Rainy heard J come out of the room. He put his hands on her shoulders. She could feel their heat through her bathrobe. She stood up and kissed him. Hadn't the decision already been made? The license just a formality, a way of providing security for the kids? Then she remembered the woman.

"Look at her," she said, pointing out the white dot of the woman's head to J.

"What's she doing?" he asked. "Why didn't you call someone?"

"She's swimming."

"What if she's committing suicide?"

"She put on a swimming cap."

"Look at those waves! There's a storm! It's midnight!"

It had never occurred to Rainy that anything was amiss. She had liked seeing the woman's white arm slicing through the dark water, her little white head turning. She had, in her own mind she realized now, even seen the woman's round mouth opening for breath.

"She's going to drown! We need to call someone!"

J turned to go back into the room, but just then shadows that were people ran towards the waves. They were waving their arms wildly, calling out, maybe the woman's name, maybe "Help!" Rainy couldn't tell because of the wind. The circles of light from the flashlights zipped around erratically like fireflies or little flying saucers. Then there was a white truck with revolving lights, lifeguards, a glowing shape of a boat out at sea, just beyond the breakers, its light jumping violently with the waves.

"Rainy," J said, shaking his head. "I can't believe you just sat here and watched her."

Rainy had imagined her swimming all the way to La Jolla. She had thought she was brave, beautiful. She had felt a kinship with her, had decided, in fact, that the woman was a sign that Rainy, too, should face the unfathomable, the unknown.

She shivered and crossed her arms. The boat had been in the same place for a long time. She wished they had binoculars so they could see. She still believed, despite all evidence to the contrary, that the woman had simply gone swimming.

"Why would you put a cap on if you were going to commit suicide?"

"Be practical for once."

"*What*?" She looked at him. Right then, she wanted to decide *not* to marry him. She wanted to be the kind of woman who never looked back.

But she was out of wine. She went back inside for a refill and a blanket. When she came out, he was sitting down. She pulled her chair next to his, he put his arm around her, she spread the blanket over both of them. The people on the beach were leaving. The boat was moving off towards the south.

"They must have found her," J said. "Just think, she could have drowned and no one would have known what happened to her."

Rainy imagined the moment when they pulled her into the boat. She was breathing hard, chilled to the bone. Shivering. From the boat, all she could see of the shore was a dark line, squares of light, which were windows, white and blue like stars, blinking. The people inside them, shadows, were conducting the ordinary business of their lives.

"Young love is trouble," Rainy said. "No matter how you look at it."

She was looking at a picture of Lydia just then and Bernadette saw on her face a kind of wistfulness, a kind of pre-grief, a sorrow of parting that made her realize the world would be an entirely different planet if she had a daughter.

"Is something wrong?" she asked.

"Sometimes I wish Lydia was a lesbian."

"Well, she might be. Not that it would make things any simpler."

"True. No simpler emotionally," Rainy said, still studying Lydia's picture, "but at least I wouldn't have to worry about AIDS or babies. Or some whacko boyfriend beating her up."

"That's what I like about you. You never sweat the small stuff."

"The other day she didn't want to go to school, and I said, 'I'm just so afraid you're going to end up in a trailer park. Working at Wendy's. Married to some asshole.'"

So they ended up in the kitchen drinking beers, talking about death, about fear, about sex—in short, about having teenagers. Maybe it was impending empty-nest syndrome. They had no way of knowing if their preoccupations were normal or apocalyptic.

"Death's the only thing that's irreversible. I keep reminding myself of that—," Rainy was on a roll, "I still remember this teacher I had who said you were lucky if someone died on you while you were young. She said we're as secretive about death as the Victorians were about sex, that death has become the great taboo."

"I lost my dad when I was young. Didn't demystify a thing." Bernadette got up and snagged an empty tuna can out of the recyclables for an ashtray. "In fact, town I grew up in, people dropped like flies. Some kind of chemical waste problem. Never made me feel secure about the unknown."

She held up a cigarette to see if Rainy wanted one, but just then Lydia walked into the room, plopped herself down on Rainy's lap. Bernadette couldn't believe she was fourteen. Already! And so tall. Like all fourteen-year-old girls, she was beautiful in a coming-into-blossom sort of way.

Lydia admonished her mother, "A little early for beer, don't you think?"

"Special occasion."

"Doesn't your Mama Bernie get a hug from her favorite girl?"

Lydia smiled, a genuine smile. "Favorite because only," she said and then, instead of hugging Bernadette, she plopped herself down in her lap. "Mama Bernie. I forgot I used to call you that."

"My God, girl, how can such a skinny little thing weigh so much?"

Lydia held up her arms and flexed her biceps. "I'm buff." Then she bounced up and down on Bernadette's lap to torture her. "So whatcha talkin' about?"

"Our favorite topics," Rainy told her.

"Sex?"

"Sex, death, love. The topics of great literature." Bernadette waved her hand through the air. "What've you been up to, my beautiful buff girl?"

"Sex and love."

"In that order?"

"Sex then. The hot sweaty variety."

Bernadette laughed. "Only kind worth having."

"It's kind of hard in the Bronco, though, cuz it's got bucket seats and the gear shift keeps getting in the way."

"Apple doesn't fall far from the tree," Bernadette raised her eyebrows.

"Okay, Mama Bernie," Rainy said.

"So that's how I was conceived? In the back of a car?" Lydia was suddenly serious.

"No, Lydia. Your dad was tall. You know that. And we didn't have a car."

Bernadette was unusually silent. There were dynamics here, tensions she had forgotten all about although sometimes Marisol did the same thing. She had a knack for bringing up the most sensitive topics in front of other people as though shaming Bernadette would make her change her mind. Or as though other people should get a vote, in, say, whether or not Marisol should have a baby. Even though, just the night before, Bernadette had thought they'd come to an agreement: *No.* No babies.

"Sor-ree. Funny how you can *do* things but you can't even talk about them."

"I should have lied." Rainy raised her eyebrows. "Love of my life. Killed in a car accident. Very neat. None of the messy complications of reality."

"Like I'd believe anything as cheesy as that."

"Really!" said Bernadette although she was thinking of something else entirely, thinking, okay, maybe she was being unfair to Marisol. "Imagine how most of us are conceived. On a night no one remembers. Maybe out of duty instead of passion. Maybe because the little chart said it was the right time."

Lydia was looking from one mother to the other. "You guys are seriously whacked."

Bernadette laughed. "No, really. Sometimes when I meet a person, I try to imagine the circumstances of their conception. Say the person is really uptight, you know, I imagine his dad was wearing striped pjs, and his mom, one of those flannel nightgowns. She's so interested in the act she's filing her nails—'*Honey*, aren't you finished yet?' 'I'm going as fast as I can, *Dear*.'"

"You've just described the conception of the principal of Lydia's
high school."

Lydia laughed. "Well, I'm going out," she stood up and hugged Bernadette.
"In the fucking Bronco with the fucker Carlos."

"As long as you're not the fuckee," Bernadette said between clenched teeth
as she lit her cigarette.

"Like I want to catch a disease." Lydia shuddered.

Rainy waited until she heard the door snap shut. "Instability or hormones?"

Bernadette laughed. "At least you guys can talk about that stuff."

"Yeah, right. I know zip about this Carlos. Zip!"

Rainy sighed and handed Bernadette a stack of pictures. "I found the film
in the bottom of a drawer last week."

They were of the kids from at least eight years earlier. It was a window into
a past Bernadette had had no part in.

"I had no idea what was on it and then, when I developed it, hello, time
travel. *Nostalgic* isn't strong enough. I felt disoriented. Lonely in advance."

Bernadette shook her head, "Man, don't I know it."

There they were: Lydia lighting the candles on the Christmas chimes;
Jesse on a skateboard, his long stocking cap trailing out behind him; Ben in
costume, a crown on his head, his mask half-white and half-black. Bernadette
had missed all of these moments and, at that particular moment, she missed
them acutely.

"I don't know them," she whispered. "Not really. Not like you and J do."

Rainy wondered at her own motives. Had she shown Berna the pictures
to wound her? A stab with a metaphoric knife? Or was it a more generous
impulse? As if in giving Berna images of that past she was, in a way, restoring
it to her, providing her with the illusion of memory. After all, even though
Rainy had lived with the kids, days in and out of peanut butter and jelly and
skinned knees and swimming lessons, she remembered very little. The past,
invariably, was a series of static images.

Bernadette sighed. She was looking at another picture of Ben. All of the
Mexican genes from J's side of the family and all of the Indian genes from
hers had coalesced in Ben—his straight, jet black hair, his eyebrows so thick
they nearly met in the middle. If Marisol had a baby, it would look like Ben.
It would be a way to reclaim time. Berna could think of it that way. And,

clearly, it wasn't fair to say no to Mari, who now, at thirty-one, could hear only the tick tick ticking. Of course, Bernadette heard the ticking, too, but in her case, she was afraid it was a time bomb counting down the minutes of her relationship with Marisol. She wasn't sure she could live in a house with small children again. She hadn't been good at it the first time. And now? To start over at forty?

Oh, love, she could hear herself say to Marisol, I can't give you any guarantees.

This was something Marisol would never understand.

This was something Rainy would never understand.

This was something even Bernadette didn't understand.

It felt like jumping off a cliff.

It felt like an act of faith.

what lydia thinks of roses

The morning after her boyfriend threatened to shoot himself, Lydia's brother had to drag her downstairs to breakfast. She was still in her boxers and sports bra, mascara smeared under her eyes. Jesse made her sit in a chair at the table and stood with his hands on her shoulders. She put her head in the crook of her arms. He started bouncing up and down on his toes, rubbing her shoulders like she was a boxer headed into a fight. "Remember, upper cut, knee to the crotch."

"Yeah, right," she moaned.

He bent his blond head over her dark one and whispered something that made her snort a laugh.

"Hey, Rainy," he said, "the girl needs substenance."

The other twin, Ben, the one who acted, according to Lydia, like he had a stick up his ass, didn't even stop chewing. "SUStenance," he said.

Lydia raised her head and gave him her drop-dead look.

"Bagel, your highness?" Rainy asked—Rainy, that's what the twins called her, since she was not Ben and Jesse's mom, only Lydia's. But they all went by the name Montoya. It was less confusing that way.

"Hey, bro," Ben said, "maybe we should take a sharp knife to school."

41

Lydia didn't flinch.

"We could show him how to use it."

Rainy said nothing. She was that kind of mom. Either distracted, or tricky, they weren't sure. Invisibility was how she got her information. She was a speck on the wall. She never intervened unless there was a chance they'd draw blood.

Jesse laughed. Egg burrito in his hand, he was on his way out the door. "Come on, Ben. We're gonna be late."

"Like it matters," Lydia said.

Ben whacked her on the head with his term paper. "Told you he was a loser."

"Did you know Ben gives the attendance lady presents?" Lydia squinted. "He has more absences than me and Jess combined."

"Imagine that." Rainy remained noncommittal. It was another of her good qualities.

"And he's *never* had to go to In-School Suspension."

"Whereas you're the Queen."

Outside, they could hear Jesse revving up the old Chevelle.

"Biggest player in the school," Ben said, making kissy kissy noises on his way out. "Tells *all* the girls he's gonna kill himself."

From upstairs, Rage Against the Machine at full blast—Lydia was pissed at someone—then the shower. She came downstairs a few minutes later wearing jeans and one of Jesse's old skater shirts, her hair still wet, no makeup. She waved a note from the attendance office in front of Rainy's face. "Just sign it." She jabbed the pen towards her mother as if it were a weapon. "Please."

"Or else what?"

Lydia rolled her eyes. "I said please."

Rainy signed it. "You know, someday you're going to have to suffer the consequences."

"I love you."

"I love you, too. Which is why I'm telling you this."

Lydia rewarded Rainy with a rare smile and then plopped down at the kitchen table. "Did you make me some tea?"

Rainy handed her a mug full of orange spice with honey and a toasted bagel, sat down across from her, coffee cup in her hands. "So the boy's using emotional blackmail."

Lydia waved her hand as if she were swatting a fly.

Rainy wished she could come up with some joke and then Lydia would laugh and confide in her. But Rainy couldn't think of one clever thing to say. Lydia was spreading her cream cheese. They were both giving it their full attention.

You are the center of my life, she wanted to say to her daughter.

Lydia stood up and went to check how she looked in the living room mirror. She drew her wet hair up into a ponytail on top of her head. A sign she actually intended to go to school? Only if Rainy was lucky. Only if that was where she planned on meeting Carlos, the *one* guy her brothers had warned her was bad news. One guy out of the whole school and she wanted him. Carlos. The sins of the mothers, Rainy ended up thinking. How she loved her daughter, this child whose skin she could no longer get beneath. That morning, Lydia's face was pensive. The sky in the window behind her, a surreal blue, the citrus trees a waxy green. When she turned away, the old mirror made her face ethereal, a Rossetti painting. She looked much sadder, just then, than any fourteen-year-old should ever look.

Lydia, Rainy sighed, my Lydia.

She knew she should say a mom thing.

She said, "I trust I will not hear from the attendance office today."

Lydia shrugged. "I *said* I'm not going to ditch."

She gathered her unopened book bag up off the couch and then blew her mother a kiss before turning and opening the front door. That's when the blue flash of the Bronco announced Carlos' arrival.

Lydia had never understood where people got the idea that girls had to be protected. They could be just as mean as boys. Meaner. That's why she hated school. Think about it. When you opened those doors, you felt like you were standing at the opening of a dark tunnel and a train made of people was coming at you full blast, they were coming at you and then rushing past you, *through* you. Too close. All noise. No air. The smell of bodies and perfume and then, if you were alone—this was why you should *never* go to school alone—some asshole would grab at your ass or your breasts and you'd have to elbow him, in the gut, if you could, but *wherever* and *hard*. It didn't matter if you got the right one because they always came in packs and, as long as you hurt one of them, when they laughed, it would be at him and not at you. But that was not the worst part. No, once you started walking down the hallway, everything slowed down. You could see the other girls watching you.

Every morning, there would be knots of three or four of them hanging out together, like they were talking, but they weren't. They weren't listening to each other. They were watching you so they could hurt you, this look on their faces, judging, checking you out, criticizing you, thinking you're fat, thinking you're ugly, thinking you don't belong, thinking they want to keep you in your place. Thinking *what* exactly? Lydia couldn't tell. She just knew it didn't matter if they were the preppy rich girls or the little wannabe gangsters or the Mexican girls from the other side who always spoke Spanish or the cheerleaders who came in all colors but always wore pink Cheerleading-is-a-Sport tee shirts, or even the Goths. They all had the same look smeared across their faces. As soon as she passed by one group, a girl would laugh or make a remark, just low enough that Lydia couldn't distinguish the words, and then the next group, alerted by the snotty laughter, would turn their heads in unison, and it would begin again.

Of course, if she were with Sandee or Xilda or Mel, the girls would drop their eyes. Xilda, who was tiny but had the temper of a chili pepper, used to confront girls who didn't look away: *You got something to say to me? Say it to my face.* Lydia kept quiet but she had perfected her *you wanna die?* look. Never drop your eyes was her motto; give no sign of submission. If she had to fight, she had to fight. Jesse had told her to go for the blouse. Rip her bra off. That's all you've got to do, he'd said, especially if you have an audience. But that was what these girls wanted to do to her, Lydia knew, expose her, some weakness in her, to humiliate her. It was what Xilda and Mel wanted to do, too, to other girls. Lydia could hear it in Xilda's laughter. It was shrill, a fist in the gut.

Then there was Amazon Kelly: her crew, the end of the morning gauntlet. For some reason Kelly wanted to kick Lydia's ass. It was all over school. Every single morning she stood outside Lydia's first-hour math class with her girls. The look on her face said, *I'm going to fuck you up, bitch.*

By the time Lydia got past Amazon Kelly into her classroom, she felt a tumor right beneath her heart, pressing down on her stomach, taking up the room for her lungs. It was hard to breathe. Plus her gut hurt. She sat in the very back row and put her head down on her desk, trying to make the feeling go away. She broke into a sweat. She needed to find a toilet. She needed to go home. She was sweating, trying to breathe, trying to make it go away, and then, inevitably, the stupid math teacher would say something to her and she would have to lift her head and look at him and shake her head, *no*, it took everything to say no, she did not know the answer.

Please, she watched his lips moving, she saw all of their heads turning, please, just leave me alone.

Which was why Lydia was glad that morning when Carlos picked her up late. By the time they got to school, everyone else would already be in class. Why this—arriving with the one guy the other girls wanted, the one guy the other guys hated—seemed to her a solution, she wasn't sure. At the time it had a kind of perverse logic. If the other girls were going to hate her anyways, they may as well have a specific reason. If the guys thought she was with Carlos, the virgin collector, as Ben called him, they would give up on thinking they could de-virginize her. But Lydia wasn't thinking even that logically. Instead, she felt as if she were simply moving towards something, not as dramatic as a moth to a flame, but the same kind of blinded, instinctual movement. Towards something. Towards *becoming*, which meant she was also moving away from who she *was*, that shy girl, the little sister self, moving outside the claustrophobic circle of the known, of her family, of her mother's constant unspoken fears, of don't don't don't, of be careful, of don't get hurt.

As she climbed into the Bronco, she wondered why she even liked Carlos. He wasn't her idea of good looking. Jesse was, with his sharp, even features, but Carlos was pretty much the opposite: big nose, brown eyes, slicked back brown hair. He did have nice big shoulders. His arms were cut. And then he spoke. And she knew. It was his voice. She loved his voice, all smooth, all low at night, the way it filled her head and she didn't feel alone. It was like one of those songs where it didn't really matter what the lyrics were, you just loved the music and the way the singing, the human voices, became a part of the whole sound and moved through you.

"Hey, Lydia," he said, "sorry about last night."

She shrugged and put in a rap tape. She knew he didn't like rap. It was Too Short, Nancy Reagan sucking on some guy's corncob and it wasn't Ronnie's. Lydia cranked it up and looked at Carlos. Her eyes said *payback time* and she knew it. And she knew he knew it. He popped the clutch and they lurched away from the curb.

Looking at his clenched jaw, Lydia was reminded of The Plan. Sandee's plan, to be exact, which, Lydia knew, was crazy—there was a *reason* Jesse called her Psycho Sandee—but the more Sandee had talked about it, the more it seemed like a possibility or, even, like fate. Like God had it all planned out. If Lydia closed her eyes, she could imagine the details. If she closed her eyes and tried to imagine another future, she saw nothing.

Sandee's logic was this: she was desperate to move in with Lydia and her family and she figured a baby would be the last straw. Her father the doctor would completely disown her. Especially if it was a black or Mexican baby and those, Sandee said, were cuter anyways. They both knew Rainy would take her in. (Rainy never said no to nobody, is the way Lydia's stepfather J—short for Javier—put it, only in Spanish, where double negatives were acceptable and triple considered emphatic.) For Lydia, The Plan was attractive because it was an alternative to school, which, no matter what she promised herself, no matter what she promised her mother, she could never make it through for even one full day. Swear to God. She felt like such a loser. She asked God for a solution: couldn't He *please* make her feel invincible? *Please*. This is what she prayed: why can't I be as stupid and oblivious as everyone else? But she knew that was impossible and so, instead, as dumb as it sounded, she had asked for a sign.

And the very next morning, as if on cue, Sandee had said, "If we both get pregnant at the same time, we'll get to drop out together when we start showing and then when the babies get born, they'll be like twins and we can stay home together and watch them."

Lydia had laughed at first but Sandee kept on painting in the details of her psycho scheme: how they would stay home together and what the babies would look like, what they would name them, how they could take them up to the park and do packets from Correspondence together. It would be way easier than going to school.

And then, like he could read her mind or something, Carlos said, "So I'm Sperm Donor Number One, huh?"

They were taking a *long* cut, out driving on the west side, on this curvy road Lydia liked a lot because you could go fast.

"What?"

The tires squealed.

"I'm Sperm Donor Number One?"

"What?"

"Sandee was telling me about your little plan. On the phone last night. She asked me if I knew anyone who would want to be her Sperm Donor."

"I suppose you volunteered."

"Fuck you, Lydia."

"First you're all telling me how sorry you are about being the Mac Daddy with Tiffany and now you're on the phone with Sandee?"

What, exactly, had Sandee said? Lydia could only imagine. He probably thought she wanted to have sex with him. What if that was where he was taking her? Somewhere to have sex? God. But what *had* she been thinking? Immaculate Conception? Not quite. Maybe she had been hoping a baby would miraculously show up in a basket on her doorstep. And her mom would let her keep it? Like a puppy or something? Fucking ridiculous.

"I heard you have a teeny-tiny-pencil dick," she wiggled her pinky finger in his face. "If I'm going to do it, I want to feel it."

As she reached into her bag for a different tape, she was thrown against the door. He was taking a curve way too fast and suddenly she could feel the Bronco slip, hear the wheels spinning out on gravel. They were sliding sideways up the shoulder, the desert going by the windshield like a movie on fast forward, all blurry and green, and the gravel flying by or else pinging as it hit the windows. Carlos' hands were clenching the wheel and this tendon was popping out of his jaw, and Lydia was thinking: Bronco's are top-heavy, Bronco's flip easy; if we flip, my mom's going to freak. She must've said that out loud because Carlos yelled, "We're NOT going to flip!"

When they finally stopped, they were headed in the exact opposite direction.

Lydia heard herself, breathless, laughing, "Think you can do that again?"

He jumped out of the car, swearing 'til she thought his hair would stand up on end. Then he started kicking all the tires. "If we have a flat, bitch, it's all your fault."

"Bitch?" She climbed out of the Bronco. "You're the one that's screaming like some little bitch." She shut the door and started walking up the road.

She wasn't planning on walking far but she figured she should make him feel bad for being such a jerk and, anyways, it was a pretty nice day—good thing it wasn't summer—the desert was pretty. All green from the rains. Lush, really. If someone dragged a body ten feet off the road, you wouldn't be even able to see it. She wondered why she always thought about things like that. She wondered why people thought the desert was barren. She wondered why being stuck out in the middle of the desert with some asshole was better than being in school.

Carlos pulled up alongside her. Just as she figured he would.

"I'm sorry, Lydia." He put on his sorriest face. "Come on, please. Get in the car."

"I'm a bitch?"

She wanted to make him squirm. She believed in punishment. She believed people should have to suffer for their sins. She didn't know how Christ could do it for everyone. The first time she'd seen Him up on the cross, she was four and it had scared the shit out of her—she'd turned the corner in this peaceful courtyard and then smack dab in the middle of these flowering bushes and leafy trees, there was a huge ten-foot cross with this guy hanging on it. He was suffering, no doubt about it. Thorns were digging into His skin and blood was dripping from His wounds. His eyes were all rolled up in His head. At first, Lydia had thought He was real, not made of wood, and she had backed away. Out of the garden. Not a good first impression of Christianity, she knew. Rainy had explained the Crucifixion but it still made Lydia wonder—if God allowed people to do that to His own son, how could He be a loving God? *A Father.* It was why she never wanted to go to church. Plus, church was full of people who were often not good themselves—those child-molesting priests, for one—and who then used Christ on the cross to scare *you* into being good. Explain that one. Christ was as good as anyone could ever be and look what had happened to Him. Going to Heaven was supposed to make up for *everything*?

She tended to believe that we suffer here on earth for what we do here on earth. Like Karma, but you don't have to wait for the next life. In a way, it was more like she and Ben and Jesse had believed when they were little. Rainy used to say bad Karma will get you in the end, but they always thought she said Carmen, Bad Carmen—like this big old mean Mexican lady was just waiting behind the bushes. One bad thought or deed and wham! she'd jump out and get you.

Which was why Lydia believed in suffering your own consequences. You'd learn better that way. Say a man beat the shit out of his kids, like Sandee's dad, he would suffer because his kids would hate him. If a girl slept around, she got called a slut. Or she got a disease. Or she got pregnant. If Carlos got hickies from one of the Tiffanys, she, Lydia, would break up with him. No matter how much he cried on the phone and threatened to shoot himself. If a friend stabbed her in the back, then she didn't trust that friend. And pretty soon, there wouldn't be a boyfriend and there wouldn't be a friendship. That was the way it worked.

"Hey, beautiful," he said, in his best AM radio voice, holding the door open for her.

She climbed in but she didn't say nothing. *Nada*. Which, when she was little, she thought was "not a"—short for "not a thing"—which just showed, she thought, how many ways there were to understand something. Even something as simple as nothing. All the way to school, she said *nada*. Not a word. She was trying to figure out how long to make him suffer.

In the parking lot, Carlos jerked the Bronco to a stop when he got to "his" space. He banged on the steering wheel. "Goddamn it! What's that piece of shit car doing there?" He threw the Bronco into reverse so fast, he killed it. He hit the steering wheel again. "Motherfucker!"

He was still pissed, all right.

Sometimes Lydia wondered about him. Oh, she knew he was used to getting his way. His dad made a lot of money. Everyone said this was his *third* car and he was only seventeen. He'd bang one up and Mommy and Daddy would buy him another one.

Of course, they were probably like that because of his older brother. Carlos was in eighth grade when it happened. He told her Steve had lived for a few minutes afterwards. He dreamed about it all the time, about the moment before, how they had been watching TV when they heard the gun. He ran in, right behind his parents, and the first thing they saw was the blood splattered on the wall behind the bed. His mom started wailing. His dad ran around the bed and held him. Carlos was the one who thought to call, but his hand was shaking so hard, he kept dialing wrong. In Carlos' dreams, he is the one who is holding Steve. In the dreams, he always has blood on his hands and, always, he wants to say something and, always, Steve wants to say something. His mouth is moving but no words are coming out. Nothing can change that.

When he talked about it, when they were alone at night in the Bronco, Lydia felt close to him. Sometimes she held him. She loved being the someone who was listening. They'd sit there and look at the splotchy lights on the windshield and kiss and kiss and he'd tell her how much he loved to talk to her and how there wasn't anyone, not one soul in the world, who meant as much to him as she did.

Which she knew was a crock but, on those nights, she let herself believe him. On those nights, she had a kind of double knowledge, like she was *in* the movie and *watching* the movie. She knew nothing was real but she still let herself pretend it was.

Plus he did know how to kiss. She had kissed only a few other guys but they'd put their whole mouth over hers and then tried to ram a fat tongue down her throat. (That alone made her think sex was probably overrated.) One kiss with them and it was over. *Later.* But not Carlos. When he kissed her, she felt it all through her body without him even touching her. What was that? Not love. She knew it wasn't love. But maybe she felt his sadness when he kissed her, his heat, as if his atoms were flowing into her and hers into him and they were connected by a kind of need. But it wasn't love. Besides, she didn't want to be *in* love with him—that would give him a kind of power over her. Nope. She wanted *him* to love *her.* No girl had been able to keep him faithful, so he was a challenge and she, Lydia Montoya, loved a challenge. She wanted to *win* the prize, not *be* the prize.

She ejected the tape, put it in her backpack, and put her hand on the door.

"Wait a minute," he said, irritably, "I haven't parked yet."

"You don't need me to park," she said.

"Wait. Lydia." Now his voice was pleading, much softer. "I meant it. What I said last night. What would I do without you?"

"I dunno. What'd you do last week?"

"You know what I mean. I don't want to *live* without you."

"That's plain sick." She opened the door and started to climb out. "Or else bullshit."

He grabbed her arm and gave her a look so sincere she thought he must have been practicing in the mirror for months. Drama, like Ben, he was into drama. This was his lovesick look. Earlier it had been his best GQ.

"I love you," he said.

But as she walked around the back of the car, she saw Amazon Kelly standing over by the door to Photo. Kelly was looking at her, a few of her girls were standing next to her, and they turned their heads in Lydia's direction. The one who was built like a brick wall laughed. Not one teacher in sight. Where was the stupid parking lot monitor when you needed him? Not over by the gate to the wrought iron fence that had been erected around the school to keep the students safe. Shit, Lydia thought, like the bad guys were on the *outside.* She continued around to Carlos' window as if that were where she'd been headed all along.

She leaned in and put her hand on his arm. "Okay," she smiled, "I can wait for you to park if you can walk me to Photo."

For Lydia, the darkroom was a place where you became invisible. You became your eyes and your hands, every part of you focused on getting your exposure right, or on burning in, or on the image emerging in the tray. Only a few people were allowed in at a time and even the most stupid among them whispered, as if they knew that to see clearly required silence. Mostly you heard the water running in the tub, a peaceful sound. It was one of the only places in school where her stomach stopped hurting. Sometimes just the smell of the chemicals could do it.

She had a print in the tray. It was hydrangea in black and white when, she thought, hydrangea *are* color, are blue-ness or violet-ness or pink-ness. Hydrangea are not line and form, which, like Rainy always said, is what black and white is all about. Of course, just below the hydrangea there was a pool of water, and light reflected on water, in black and white, can become shape and form. It was awesome. The hydrangea were these gray blurs, especially indistinct and grainy because of the color negative, but below them, the light on the water came out like a gray and white abstract, the edges sharper than the flowers but still out of focus.

Lydia had known it would be scratchy—it was such an old negative—but the blurs and the grainy stuff, even the tiny scratches, all those flaws were what she liked about it. It reminded her of the way memory feels.

Then the photography teacher came up behind her. She could feel his breath on her neck before he even spoke. She moved away, quickly, bumping the tray, sloshing the fixer. Didn't old guys know they were creepy?

"No true blacks and whites," he said. "Are you using a color negative? You can't get any clarity with a color negative."

God. He couldn't even wait until she got it out of the tray? But she wasn't about to tell him a color negative was all she had. What? She was supposed to fly up to Washington to get a black-and-white shot of Gram's garden?

"If I had wanted a black-and-white negative," she told him, "I would've bought black-and-white film."

Not what he wanted to hear.

So after it came off the dryer, Lydia put it in her notebook and decided not to submit it in her portfolio. Did she really want him putting it up as an example of what *not* to do? She hid it in her notebook and then after lunch, in fifth hour, when the stupid blonde from the Knock Me Over and Fuck Me Crew started talking about how many guys wanted to do her, Lydia could open the notebook, jam her fists over her ears, and meditate on Gram's garden: there she'd be, seven years old, taking pictures with the ancient 35-

millimeter Rainy had bought at a yard sale, looking through the viewfinder at clouds, while these big poof balls of color were waving above her head and the sky was in the water.

That's what she loved, really, there was nothing you could see on this slick white piece of paper and then you put it in the tray and swirled the developer over it with your fingers and then, as if your fingers were magic, *something* just seemed to grow out of nothing. Trees, people, sky, dogs, a piece of your life. Wait too long, it all turned black.

Lydia looked around for Jesse when she got to open gym. A bunch of guys had already started warming up. The cheerleaders had gathered in one corner. One of them was Tiffany, the girl Carlos had been with on the weekend. Tiffany looked at Lydia and tossed her hair. Lydia wanted to ask her why she thought it was such an honor to suck a guy's dick.

She remembered Carlos' face the night she had let him unbutton her shirt. I want to look at you, he'd said, we don't have to do anything. She could still feel his hands running down her neck, over the top of her bra, his fingers leaving little trails of fire wherever he touched her. She knew, if she ever slept with him, it would be all over school in a heartbeat. But she had wanted to. Well? he'd said and he was looking at her like he was In Love. He tugged on the front clasp of her bra. But she'd said no. The look on his face, she knew he would consume her.

Where was Jesse? She didn't want to stand around like she didn't have anything better to do. If he didn't show up pretty soon, she'd go looking for Sandee.

Just then Ramon yelled from mid-court. "Hey, Montoya!"

She looked around for her brothers, but Ramon meant her, and so she went out on the court. She could hit the three, easy, had a great outside shot, and she wasn't afraid of playing with guys—nobody would play her as hard as her brothers. Ben used to throw the ball *at* her face and he never got in trouble because it was a *game*. And once, her front tooth broke when it collided with Jesse's elbow on a rebound. Plus she had played on boys' teams at the Y since forever.

This afternoon, they were passing a few balls around, making shots. She passed to Ramon and he went up for a lay-up and then this short black guy bounce-passed it back to her. She made a three. Swish. All net. She liked this better than an actual game. It moved faster, was all motion, had its own rhythms when they could keep the ball in play. She was driving for the basket and somebody slipped the ball right out from under her hand. Jesse. That was his move. She and Ben and Jesse had played together so much that they could read one another's minds, pass without eye contact. He passed it back to her, she went up for a jump shot and, suddenly, she was seeing stars. Someone had fouled her bad. When Jesse helped her up off the floor, a couple of guys were standing around, absolutely quiet, chagrined, but that wasn't what Lydia noticed. She didn't care who stuffed her. It was Tiffany, she heard, Tiffany laughing. Tiffany was pointing at Lydia and laughing. Carlos was standing next to her on the sidelines.

A guy standing next to Lydia said, "We hear they're real." He was looking at her chest. "Cool."

"Yeah, Montoya," another guy said, "your body's boomin'."

When Lydia walked out of sixth hour, Sandee was waiting for her. "You'll never guess what he got you!"

Lydia ignored her. She wanted to catch a ride with Jesse.

"Come on," Sandee pulled on her hand. "I'll give you a hint. They're red."

Lydia turned the corner to the east parking lot and saw Jesse leaning against his primer-gray Chevelle. He was talking to Carlos whose back was to her. Everyone was milling around. Tiffany was unlocking her car. It was going to rain.

"I went with him and picked them out," Sandee said.

Just then, Ben walked up behind Carlos and picked him up off the ground. He twirled Carlos around. "You wanna be dead, I can arrange it."

A group of guys had gathered. Maybe they thought it would be a fight, but when Ben saw Lydia, he dropped Carlos so fast he nearly fell. Ben laughed maniacally. Like it was all the biggest joke.

"See?" Sandee said.

Carlos had a dozen long-stemmed roses in his arms. Red.

Red roses.

So Carlos thought he could play her. And he thought he could do it in front of the whole school. She felt everyone's eyes pushing at her. She was pinned under glass. Some dead butterfly. A bug.

He held out the roses. "I didn't say anything about you. Honest."

She took them.

I bet he loves her someone in the group of guys snickered. *I love you. Say it, you pussy. I love you. I can't live without you.*

Lydia gave a rose to Ben. She gave a rose to Jesse. She smiled at Carlos and gave one to Sandee.

The clouds were gray and pushing down. She gave a rose to Ramon, she gave a rose to a Mexican cowboy in a black hat.

"Heartless," he said.

She even gave a rose to Tiffany, the skank, who was standing with her mouth hanging wide open.

Appropriate, Lydia thought.

Amazon Kelly and her girls were walking by, gawking. Carlos looked stricken. Lydia expected him to go ballistic. He went ballistic about everything.

Not this.

There were six more roses. Lydia took one and crushed it in her hand and then opened her fingers, let the petals drop on the ground. She did the same thing, slowly, methodically, to each of the last five roses. There were petals everywhere, petals falling all over the parking lot. Red petals. Petals scattering away in the wind.

"That," Lydia said to Carlos, "is what I think of roses."

emily's exit

My older sister Emily practiced suffering as if it were an art form. She liked the clean lines of pain and would often lie, arms folded over her chest, as if she were dead or dying. Long hair held back by a wide black headband, a large silver cross on her chest, she looked like nothing so much as a nun, although if you'd asked her, she would have said that Catholicism was corrupt. No mystery or mysticism for her. No metaphors, thank you. The word of God was in the Bible and all you had to do was believe it.

Even her bedroom was spare and fundamental, a line drawing in progress. Danish, that's what she liked. When she was eighteen, Emily had insisted our mother remove all the antiques she'd spent years refinishing—cherry dresser, four poster bed, oak rolltop desk—and replace them with the sparest, geometric furniture she could find until all of Emily's room had sharp edges. Light wood, sculptural shapes, tubular lamps, a woven mat to cover the wooden floor. Blinds, not curtains. No comfort. When I looked in her room, I froze. I felt like I was in some icy Ingmar Bergman film—white, black, and tan with a few red accents pulsing.

Emily lying straight-backed on her hard bed, arms folded across her chest. Was she asleep or pretending? Her bed was never rumpled. Perhaps she slept without breathing, I always wondered. Above the bed, one of her own drawings, as simple as the sparest Matisse. A few curved lines suggesting a face, crescent-moon eyes, lifted, of course, toward the Lord. Two lines, which were hands pressed together in prayer, intersecting two shorter lines, which were lips, also pressed together. A cross. Silencing her.

"Emily?"

This was the last time I would see her before she disappeared.

"Emily?"

She opened her eyes.

"Dinner's ready."

Little did I know she was emptying herself to see if God would enter.

Of course, my vision of her is tainted and diminished by time, reduced to the most essential details. She disappeared into the Sonoran Desert to the south of us when I was sixteen. She was twenty and headed, I guess, for her own brand of sainthood. Why else make the trek across the desert in June?

Emily knew the desert. Perhaps the geometry of it appealed to her. The sloping curve of hills on the horizon, angular volcanic outcroppings to the west, the smooth disks of the prickly pear, phallus of saguaro, the long skinny fingers of the ocotillo, crooked elbows of cholla. Everything pierced by spikes and thorns. Earth, caliche, hard and parched, dry sand, no water, that was the desert to the south of here. Forbidding and hostile. It was not the lush desert full of mesquite and palo verde we grew up in. No. That would've been too easy for Emily.

And June? In other parts of the country, June might be June moon spoon, long walks in the pastoral twilight, damp evening air cool and fragrant with alfalfa, but June in Arizona is one word: hot. Hold your hand over the burner to feel the way the sun sears the skin at noon. Waves of heat radiate up from the asphalt, even from bare earth. Dry June air bakes the tissues of your lungs when you inhale. June light bleaches the color out of the mountains and sky; even mesquite leaves fade to a dull gray and wilt. Midnight is a dark furnace. Everything, everyone waits for the clouds to build in the sky, for the monsoon rains, for relief. June is stasis. Limbo. Only the cicadas, in their incessant chirping, move.

They say the Apache could run through the desert all day without water. They'd disappear into it, then reappear like a mirage. That was how I imagined Emily's exit. She just began walking into the wilderness of the desert and, as she walked, she slowly faded until she disappeared altogether. Like a camera trick. Fade out. Perhaps she held a small, blue stone in her mouth and from it sprang forth a trickle of cool water, a miracle stone, that's what she would have needed.

But it couldn't have been easy. Emily was no Apache. She knew the gruesome details, how every summer, poor Mexicans fried to death in the desert: their thirst compelling them to drink their own urine, the sun so hot it boiled their brains inside their skulls, their tongues swollen black, their bones eventually picked clean and bleached white. Surely the irony of her crossing, of going against traffic, occurred to her.

When Emily disappeared, my mother, an ex-hippie who wore Birkenstock sandals with wool socks no matter what the season, occasion, or rest of her outfit demanded, became a Buddhist. It was the only way she could deal with it, she said. Emily's room became a shrine where my mother would retreat when she was feeling stressed. I'd hear the bell and know a clear space was opening up in her heart, a space she was making calm and quiet so she could get a transmission from Emily.

After a few months of not-knowing, my mother decided to build a garden for meditation in the back yard. Maybe she thought it was too difficult for Emily's spirit to come in through the walls of the house. At any rate, she mortared stones together to make a small pool and fountain; she made a tiny shrine on one side of the pool and planted small palms, weird cacti that looked like they were from outer space, and other geometric plants Emily would have liked. It had the same ascetic quality as Emily's room and often, when I stood in the window of our air-conditioned house and watched my mother meditate in her garden, it would occur to me that Emily was more real to her than I was. I was the child who was never missed and not grieved, who paled in her physical realness while Emily began to glow incandescently in her absence.

Shortly after the garden was built, Emily began to visit our mother in the middle of the night, like a vision. She'd float through the air to her, surrounded like *la Virgen de Guadalupe* with tongues of light, and then pause right before my mother's eyes and say, "I am whole."

"I swear," my mother used to say to me the next morning over coffee and a bagel, her eyes moist with gratitude for Emily's thoughtfulness, "it wasn't a dream. It was her and there was this glowing light all around her. It wasn't a dream, it was her spirit, she came to me, and I was filled with warmth and a feeling of complete well-being."

One morning, after the umpteenth vision, I couldn't help it. I said, "Maybe she said, 'I'm a *whore*,' not I'm *whole*. That's why she has to keep coming back. Because you don't listen. You never listen."

My mother was not amused. "That's it," she glared at me. "You've always been jealous."

But jealousy wasn't my problem and she knew it. Emily and I had always been on two different trajectories. For as long as I could remember, Emily had tortured herself by trying to figure out what God wanted from her. She couldn't even eat a candy bar without His blessing. Okay, that might be an exaggeration, but if one could flagellate the spirit; that's what Emily did. Lying still on her bed, she took out some interior cat-o'-ninetails and flailed away. What had she said that might offend the Lord that day? What were her impure thoughts? What scripture should she turn to? And when she had driven her own voice from inside her head and another voice entered, she was never sure if it was the voice of God or the devil.

On those days, she was so weak she could scarcely crawl from bed. We would bring her water, juice, vegetable broth, lift her head to help her drink. My mother bought air purifiers, removed yet more objects from the room, drew the blinds lest the light motes contained something undetectable by anything less sensitive than Emily's spirit. The doctors were perplexed, one specialist said perhaps she was allergic to certain chemicals or gasses in the atmosphere around her, but I knew it was paralysis. Emily wanted so badly to believe God had chosen her that she would bring suffering upon herself to prove it.

The way I tortured myself was much simpler. I carved the names of boys I liked into my thigh with a razor blade. If Emily's domain was the spirit, mine was the flesh.

Not long after my mother had finished building her shrine, we got a visit from Emily's boyfriend. He wanted to know if we'd heard from her. Rick—that was his name—was a revelation. We hadn't known Emily had a boyfriend, for one thing, and for another, I would have thought, had she had one, his name would've been Meshack or Esau or Obediah or one of those other so-and-so-begat-so-and-so names. But, no, he was *Rick*, a regular guy, baseball cap, majoring in business management, drove a little red truck and ate at

McDonald's. They'd met one another at church, so he was a Christian but, as he would later tell me, not devout enough for her.

His appearance was, in some ways, a setback for my mother. At that point, we didn't know Emily had disappeared into the desert. My mother had assumed, wrongly, that either Emily had finally been overcome by passion and run off with the love of her life—as my mother had done at her age, mistaking the summer of love for the real thing—or that she had run off with a group of evangelists and was trailing some preacher around the country, much in the same way my mother had trailed the Grateful Dead. Either way, my mother had cherished the idea that Emily was following, if only vaguely, in her footsteps and was off on a trek to find herself.

 Rick's appearance disabused her of the first notion and of some others as well. It seems my sister not only had a secret amour (sans sex, of course) but she had invented a secret life (sans my mother and me). She'd told everyone at church that her parents were missionaries in Indochina and she had grown up there surrounded by infidels. She'd told Rick my mother was her crazy sinning aunt and her parents had sent her here to save her soul. She had never mentioned me: I was not a sister left back on some island, nor was I the sinning aunt's sinning daughter. I did not exist in her invented universe. I was not even worth a lie.

What was it that plunged my mother into despair? That she didn't know Emily? The thought that the heart and mind of her own flesh and blood was foreign to her? This was Emily, the daughter she had created inside herself when everyone was advising an abortion; Emily, her oldest, the one she had sacrificed her own hopes and education for. To hear her tell it, she had given up everything: Emily's father because he was dealing, peace marches, smoking dope, dropping acid, grooving with the Dead and the Airplane (because, after all, she had lived in the Haight). No, that scene was getting too weird, violent, and so she had opted for motherhood as activism, nurturing life in a world bent on destroying it. And now, now, not only was Emily foreign and mysterious, but closed. Willfully closed. My mother's heart was broken. The ringing of the bell in Emily's room didn't help. The cooing of the mourning dove in the garden didn't heal. The space cleared in her heart was not expectant. It was empty.

While my mother was busy retreating inside herself, trying to undo the knots of Emily's betrayal, I was busy snooping. The advent of Rick motivated me to search even harder for the elusive journal I was sure Emily had kept. Sure enough, I finally found it stashed in a box marked "Fishing Gear" on the top shelf in the storage room. In excruciating detail, her love aflame: Rick's eyes locking on hers when she was supposed to be deep in prayer; in meetings, his hand brushing against hers made spasms in her heart; the heat from his breath as he sang hymns was like the summer wind. Who could have known Emily was filled with such passion? The problem was, she wanted to be filled with *com*passion, in the Biblical sense, as in filled with the passion of Christ.

She asked God for a sign. She emptied her heart, her mind, for God—but Rick kept entering. His voice, his smell, his skin. He was distracting her from Christ. His reassurances of love and fidelity were like whispers from the devil himself. And when she gave in, let him hold her, felt the heat of his body through his shirt, felt his breath in her hair, his lips on her forehead, then she knew she couldn't trust him. Every molecule in her body was saying yes. Sin, sin, sin. It was so clear. Rick was the way of sin, and everyone knew what the wages of sin were.

No wonder she took off through the desert: she wanted to deny the body, to scourge it with heat and thirst, to vaporize her flesh and become air, spirit.

But if the desert was Emily's test, then I was Rick's. It was inevitable that, under the blade of my razor, little bloody *Ricks* would begin blossoming on my thighs before I went to bed each night.

Only when María showed up did we realize what had really happened to Emily. In Spanish, sprinkled with equal parts Spanglish and broken English, María told us that Emily had been found lying in the desert hills near the small town of Magdalena in Sonora, Mexico. She was past delirious—in fact, they'd thought she was dead at first—her lips so parched they were cracked open, her body temperature off the thermometer. And, sure enough, María said, when Emily woke up, she was *muy disorientado*. Knew not where she was, nor who she was, nor why she didn't know. When she opened her eyes, it was as if she were still asleep or dreaming. She didn't seem to see anyone who was in the room, was staring instead at some interior apparition. She didn't seem to hear or understand what anyone said to her and, when she tried to speak, all that came out was fragments of prayers. It was as if *she* were not there. María was sure she was possessed. "*No hay nadia pa'dentro,*" she said. "Very creepy."

Emily had been taken by the men who found her in the hills to the hacienda where María worked. It was owned by a strange *rubia*, or blonde woman, the daughter of a wealthy Spaniard who was not all there herself. In fact, according to María, this woman was *muy loca*. It happened when she lost both of her children in a car accident. They were on their way to visit her when their car rolled three times, killing them both instantly. After a period of intense grief, where *la señora* shut herself up in one wing of the house and refused to see anyone, she emerged dressed all in white and like *la llorona* herself, floated down the halls of the hacienda in an unworldly calm. She had the bodies of both children exhumed and, just as Father Kino's bones lie in a glass case in the town square of Magdalena, the partially decomposed bodies—María shivered and crossed herself—of *los niños de la señora* lie in their own glass cases in the central courtyard of the hacienda.

As soon as Emily had recovered, every morning she and *la señora* would kneel and pray before the caskets of the dead children. This alarmed María so much that she went through Emily's things, found her I.D. and decided she must find out if she had a family.

"If you don't go down there, she will be lost to you." That's what she told my mother. "*La señora* keeps her up late at night, every night, praying. When she starts to fall asleep, she wakes her up. Sometimes she doesn't let her eat. They spend all day together, sitting in the garden, reading the Bible, praying in the chapel. Always your daughter has to stay at *la señora's* side." She shook her head and whispered. "Sometimes she opens the glass and makes your daughter kiss her daughter's hand. *Aye, Díos mío.*" She crossed herself. "It isn't natural."

No surprise, then, when my mother loaded María and a few of her things into her old Volvo and headed for Magdalena. I immediately called Rick and told him I had news about Emily and, *voila!*, he hopped in his little red truck and was standing on my doorstep in no time.

He had on a white tee shirt, blue jeans, no baseball cap. His hair was cut short and I knew, under the palm of my hand, just what his head would feel like. His eyes were hazel and while, on the way over, they may have been visualizing Emily, once I opened the front door and smiled at him, he only had eyes for me—and, in them, I could see: I was as luscious as a peach.

Now I am not saying Rick was a man of few convictions and I am not saying I seduced him because Emily had erased me. Both of those things may be true, of course, to some extent, but all I know is what happened. Not why.

All I know is that I stepped forward. I put my hand on his cheek and I said, "Rick. I don't think Emily's coming back."

"Where is she?" he asked and, as I watched his lips move, I could see why he had become her personal demon.

"Over the edge," I told him. "For sure."

I took his hand and led him into the house, taking him on a little impromptu tour. First we visited Emily's room. We sat on her hard bed and I told him all about the crazy *señora* in Magdalena and how Emily was kissing the bony hand of a dead girl.

He seemed sad. Still, I wanted him to sit there for a moment, in that room, so he could clearly remember the facts of Emily, her arid surfaces, the edges of her fear. The way she would never be able to give in to this messy life.

Then I led him into my room. The soft rumpled bed, the feather pillows you could plump up and then sink into, the fat plum-colored comforter, the window full of green leaves and sunlight. We sat next to each other on the bed. He sighed. I put my arm around him. "I'm sorry," I told him.

I put the palm of my hand against his head and rubbed his skull. I loved the downy texture of his hair, the bristles on his cheek where he hadn't shaved yet. I knew his chest would be smooth, there would be a line of hair above his belly button.

He looked at me. "She was so pure of heart," he said, but he didn't mean it. That's not why he was sad.

I just smiled. I put my other hand on his knee.

"I'm not," I said.

As if it were a sigh, we fell back onto the bed together. For a while we just lay there. We sighed. We were quiet. Emily had left an absence in each of us.

Then he leaned over me and said, "I know you're not Emily. I'm glad."

He kissed me and I put my arms around his neck and felt myself rise to meet him. We began comforting each other over the loss of her, and while it healed me (in certain ways) to feel him as she never would, I was also thinking how she was right: two people can't complete one another. One person can't fill the holes in another's heart. For an instant, I became her and I was terrified by her knowledge: nothing could ever fill my essential alone-ness.

My mother returned without her, just as I had predicted she would. She said the hacienda was a beautiful place, an oasis set back in the hills of the desert. The high white walls had disturbed her, at first, because it looked like a fortress, a fortress from which Emily would never escape. But then, she sat me down and took both my hands in hers. "It isn't a matter of escape," she said. In a way, my mother's worst fear had come true. Emily was not herself. Maybe the heat had boiled her brain, maybe she had hit her head when she fell from exhaustion, but she no longer spoke much English. She was wan and timid as if she were much younger in some ways, but her eyes seemed ancient, my mother said, they shone with fever or with some unworldy wisdom.

"She is not the same person," my mother shrugged. "I don't know. Maybe she saw something or something happened in the desert that changed her. But," and here she covered her heart with her hand, "she barely recognized me. It was as if she hadn't seen me for years. For us, it's been months. For her, a lifetime."

She went on to tell me that when she first arrived, Emily had seemed frightened of her. She'd clung to *la señora* as if she were a child. When my mother held out a picture of me, Emily had smiled and said I was pretty. *Simpatica*. But when my mother asked her if she wanted to come home, she started quaking and crying. She seemed to believe that if she stepped over the threshold of the hacienda, out into the desert, she would fall off the face of the earth and go straight to hell.

"There was nothing I could do to reassure her," my mother said. She said Beatrice, that was *la señora's* name, could not reassure Emily either, and so my mother had come home alone.

My mother had said nothing about the dead children in the courtyard. And she never did. Ever. She retreated into her room and grieved. For a few months afterwards, she toyed with the idea of visiting again, of sending psychiatrists to Mexico, doctors, priests, preachers. Who could best untangle the mysteries of Emily's mind? My mother couldn't decide. She seemed to lose her will. She spent hours in Emily's room, hours in the garden. She turned inward, like Emily had, trusting that some vision would come and liberate her from her own indecision.

Finally, on the anniversary of Emily's exit, she showed me a picture taken in the garden of the hacienda. It was true, Emily's eyes burned with a fever I'd never seen in them. She was a different version of herself, at once paler and yet more intense, as if the flame of her spirit was consuming her flesh from the inside. Then my mother showed me photographs of the *retablos* Emily had been painting for *la señora*. They were beautiful, not the primitives that most *retablos* were. Instead, in hers, the Madonna and Child had delicate faces, elongated bodies, gauzy, ethereal gowns. They were otherworldly, Byzantine in their simplicity and grace.

She said, "Emily has chosen."

Of all the things in the Bible, the Song of Solomon was the only book I ever liked. Sometimes, in the afternoons when Rick and I were in my room, I would look out the window and see my mother in her garden and realize she was turning ever more inward, seeking some sort of Nirvana which was *in* this world although not *of* it. Then I would think of Emily, how she had entered another world altogether.

Sometimes, when Rick touched me or as my hands wandered over him, I would remember phrases. It was as if his body held a kind of Braille that only my fingers could read and I'd remember the song: this is my beloved, this is my friend, his mouth is most sweet, his eyes as doves, his cheeks a bed of spices, his lips like lilies. And I'd think how it was true, our bed was green. And how, if there was a God, He had made the fruits of this world so sweet, so sweet it was some kind of sin, maybe the worst kind of sin, to turn your back on them too soon.

phoenix

Not even June and it was a dog-dancing day. Asphalt sticky as gum. Gloria had heard it was so hot in Phoenix that rubber gaskets were melting, windshields falling out; some were simply shattering as the glass expanded from the heat. Birds were probably passing out in the trees. Electricity use spiking off the grids. If the cicadas would give it up for one minute, if traffic would come to a halt, she was sure she'd be able to hear the pumps sucking the artesian wells dry. Then Tucson would collapse into the hollow earth left behind. It was that hot, apocalyptically hot, hot enough to believe the sun could fry her and everyone else like so many grasshoppers in a cast-iron skillet.

She shut her eyes and saw red, held her arms out so her pits wouldn't stain her linen blouse. Dammit. She had been afraid the car would overheat and so she'd turned it off, stood in the only shade she could find, waiting for her daughter. The bell rang and the kids flooded out of the dirty brick buildings. No Danika. There was her friend, skinny café olé Jamie, a halfie like Dan—though Dan was half Mexican and half white. Greek to be precise. (Of course, that was the half Gloria worried about.)

In fact, Danika's resemblance to her father scared the shit out of Gloria.

Dan had always looked like him, especially her green eyes and the way she moved her hands—she had been born with a pencil in her hand. Doodled constantly, faces made of thick curving lines, eyes the shape of dolphins. Long narrow noses. Mouths like birds in flight. She had his dark moods and even some of his facial expressions, even though she had seen him, what, maybe three times in her whole life? It made Gloria wonder if memory was at least partly physical, if, for instance, Dan retained a memory of him deep in her blood and bones, a kind of genetic doom and gloom. God, she hoped that wasn't the case.

Jamie, a gregarious girl now that her anti-depressants had kicked in, started waving wildly once she saw Gloria.

"Oooooh, that Jamal is so fine." She tilted her head in his direction so Gloria could check him out. She smiled an impish grin. "But Mexicans can be fuckable, too."

"Oh," Gloria laughed, "glad to hear it. Equal Opportunity being an amendment and all."

She prided herself on being hip, but, so help her, she didn't think she'd ever get over the way Danika's friends talked. Fuckable. Fuck me with a chain saw. Bite me. Suck me. Had feminism accomplished nothing?

Gloria watched the kids stream by, burn their fingers on the chrome handles of their cars, stand with the doors open, fanning the hot air from outside into the even hotter oven of the car.

Still no Danika.

Where was she? Gloria looked at her watch. She had to be at the gallery, in Phoenix, at six. *Before* the opening at seven. Leave it to Dan to completely forget. It would be nice to have time to eat first. The last thing she needed was these nerves on an empty stomach.

Jamie shrugged. "She was in first hour, but I didn't see her at lunch."

Gloria scanned the lot.

"Usually we eat lunch together," Jamie said. "Maybe she went off campus today."

"She'd be back by now." Gloria had given up on arguing about attendance. Long ago. She just hoped Dan would make it through her senior year.

Jamie shrugged.

The wind came up. Like a blast of hot air from a furnace. If Gloria had one drop of sweat on her skin, the wind might have cooled her off, but in this heat the moisture evaporated before it reached the surface. It evaporated in advance.

"I suppose she went some place with Joshua."

"He got busted for having a knife in his backpack the other day."

"Great." Gloria pictured a hunting knife. She gave Jamie a look: *Yes? What else?*

"But it was just a pocket knife so they didn't suspend him."

"God, Jamie. Thanks for scaring me half to death."

"He's *such* a puss," she snorted. "He would never *do* anything."

And then Gloria saw her daughter, walking by herself, between the buildings. On her way over from the other parking lot. She was walking alone. She never liked to go anywhere alone. Like all the other kids, Gloria knew, Danika believed in traveling with an entourage. Safety in numbers. But she was walking alone across the parking lot, striding through the waves of heat, the wind whipping her long ponytail out, her backpack slung across her shoulder like she was a time traveler emerging out of a wasteland.

Danika got into the car without acknowledging either Jamie or Gloria. She cranked the AC and the music up full blast—she always did that when she didn't feel like talking—and they drove to the center where Jamie was volunteering.

"Check it out, *chica*," Jamie was saying, "I'm telling you. Fine dudes come in here all the time."

"Condition of their probation?" Gloria asked.

Dan shot her a look.

"That is Tyrone's car." Jamie wiped her chin to get rid of the metaphoric drool. "Get me a bucket!"

Dan scrunched up her shoulders. Not impressed. Twisted her hair up on top of her head. "Maybe tomorrow," she caught Jamie's hand and squeezed it.

As they turned on to the street, Dan put a tape in. Gloria wanted to say, "Well? Where were you?" But she pressed her lips together. Bit her tongue. Said nothing. She drove. She was waiting for a confession.

Danika was thinking about a questionnaire she and Jamie had come up with: *Before You Let Him Get in Your Pants*—at least that's what Jamie had wanted to call it. They thought it might count as extra credit for Health; after all, it did have something to do with human development. It went like this:

Are you currently married?

If not, do you have a steady bitch?

If no or yes, how many hos on the side?

How many times do you think you're a father?

Have you ever used a condom?

Do you know what one is?

Do you think they make one big enough for you?

Have you ever been arrested or convicted of a felony?

How many times of a misdemeanor?

How many substances do you abuse on a regular basis?

How many substances do you abuse, period?

Do you have a steady job?

Is it legal?

They thought the health teacher could make the list available as a public service. Maybe publish it some place. Some girls were just dumb enough to need it.

Jamie, for instance, Danika thought, as she watched her friend enter the center. She hoped Jamie would remember to use it when Tyrone made his smooth move—or, more likely, when Jamie threw herself at him, like she had with the guy next door. She'd put on a red teddy and high heels. It was the middle of December and she'd gone outside, stood next to his car while he was working on it, her hips swaying, fingers snapping: *jingle bell, jingle bell, jingle bell…* like a sleazy lounge singer.

God, Danika wished she could have seen it.

She looked at her mom, imagined her laughing at the questionnaire. She could probably add a few questions of her own—but why was she was all dressed up? Her new linen blouse, hair in a French twist, new skirt, kicky, is what she'd called it at the mall. She didn't usually dress like that for teaching. Shit. Danika had forgotten. The gallery opening in Phoenix. Her mom's portfolio was on the back seat. Danika wondered if she'd made her mom late. Not the right time to regale her with the list, she guessed. Timing was everything. If she read the questions to her now, her mother would just raise her eyebrow and say, "Why are any of those things even part of the landscape?"

Danika turned down the music. "I'm starving," she said.

The guy behind the counter, probably a university student, was extremely attentive. Danika acted as if she didn't even notice but, on the way out to the car, she jabbed her mom with her elbow and said, "Now *he* was hot." In the car, when she opened the bag with her sandwich, she found a phone number and the word "party" written on the napkin. She turned red. "Do you think he meant to give this to me?"

"Well, I don't have one in mine," Gloria said. It was hard to believe that Danika didn't know how beautiful she was. Didn't see her clear olive skin, her full lips, her green eyes flecked with gold as remarkable. Saw, instead, the gaps between her teeth, her feathery eyebrows, freckles across her nose. Well, Gloria supposed, it was just as well. "And how do you think that makes me feel?" she asked.

Danika laughed and then shrugged. "Like an old granny with saggy boobs and her stockings slipping down around her ankles."

"No, worse. Like one of those doctor's wives with the dimply thighs. You know, khaki shorts, alligator shirts, sensible shoes." Gloria unwrapped her sandwich and spread a napkin across her skirt. "I never could figure out why guys with money pick women like that."

"Cuz they're nerds," Danika said, her mouth full, "or cuz they screw around."

Speaking of which, Gloria thought.

"I didn't go to all of my classes today."

"Do tell," Gloria said. She started the car. Looked in the rearview. A dust devil. It nearly knocked a guy right off his motorcycle.

"It's a long story, Mom."

"I bet."

"Joshua and I got into this big fight. Outside his English class and everyone in the class was looking at us, so we were going to go out to his car to talk but then we saw the security guard and so we took off."

"And?"

"We went out to his house."

"And?"

"He wouldn't bring me back to school. He was being a dick."

His family lived way out in the middle of the desert, Gloria knew that much.

"His dad was there, so we went and ate breakfast at a restaurant and then, when we went back, his dad was gone."

"I don't understand why he wouldn't bring you back to school."

Danika very patiently finished chewing the bite she had in her mouth.

Gloria waited.

"What about the word *dick* don't you understand?"

"So Joshua was being a dick. Imagine that. But, still, you went out to breakfast with him? And then you went back to his house?"

"I hate it when you make me look stupid."

"And I don't know why you can't do what you're supposed to do."

Danika took a wrinkled-up cigarette out of her backpack. Lit it, arched her long neck and blew the smoke towards the roof of the car.

"They're your lungs." Gloria rolled her eyes. She was not going to react.

"Joshua hates it when I smoke."

"What a concept. Ruin your health to get back at him."

"Ha. Ha."

It was a dangerous situation, Gloria thought, no matter how you looked at it. All you had to do was walk in a room with the two of them in it and you got zapped by the sexual ions sizzling through the air. Sometimes, when Gloria looked at them, she panicked; she wanted to lock Danika in a high, round dungeon. Other times she simply longed to be young again and in love—even though it had been the most painful time of her life. There was something about the intensity of those emotions, something fundamental and essential, you could feel every molecule in your body, you knew you were alive. You *were* your body and your connection to him was both purely physical and transcending the physical; it was the place where sexuality, your body, becomes who you are, spirit and energy. Desire.

She remembered Nick leaning towards her, his green eyes, it was like drowning. When he was with other girls, that was a different kind of drowning. His depressions, that was another kind. She had loved him for almost four years—until she found herself pregnant with Danika—but she had never forgotten the longing, that pure desire, the abandon with which you can give yourself over to the other without question at that age. It never happens again. Never.

Eighteen when she fell for Nick. Only one year older than Danika. Maybe that's what scared her. How long had she and Joshua been out at his house? They were arguing. No one was home. He wouldn't let her leave. Until what? What did this mean? Did Gloria really think they'd had sex for the first time? No. She was sure she would have felt it. Physically. Her body would have told her. Her symbiosis with Danika was that strong and, in some ways, she was afraid it kept her from being a good mother. She couldn't separate her feelings

74

from Danika's, couldn't make objective decisions.

It was a big house, surrounded by desert, long dirt roads leading to the main road. The creosote out there was as tall as a man, there were Palo Verdes, mesquite, jumping cholla. They were surrounded by this lush desert and they were in the house, arguing. She imagined Danika there: she felt trapped, she was trailing her hand down the white wall, "Take me back to school."

"No," he grabbed her by the shoulders. "Not until you listen."

Joshua was the jealous kind and Danika knew how to push his buttons.

But Gloria suddenly realized this: Danika had been in complete control. He didn't take her back to school because she wasn't ready to leave.

Gloria sighed. Today of all days. And why Danika had insisted on going to the gallery in Phoenix with her, she wasn't sure.

"I hate it when you sigh like that."

"I hate it when you try to manipulate me."

"Why do you have to start being a bitch?"

"Why didn't you call me for a ride?"

"*Mom*." Huge sigh. "Like you could've left school anyways."

"Well, was he pushing you around?"

"Like he wants to die." She tossed her head. "Just because *you* got pregnant doesn't mean I will. *I'm* going to make my *own* mistakes."

Danika didn't want to talk any more. She leaned her face against the window and watched through slit eyes as the landscape, made even more flat and colorless by the strong light, streamed by. Off in the distance, low mountains slumbered like blue dinosaurs. Yucca plants, which had always reminded her of dwarfed and deformed palm trees, straggled by the side of the road. The freeway was much better at night. Not the scenery, because who cared about that, but its flatness, the lack of cars at that time. You could really open a car up. She and Josh had done that before, had driven nearly all the way to Phoenix at least a couple of times, just to keep moving. One night he had let her drive. It was raining, just slightly, a mist, just enough to cool the air. They had rolled down the windows and she had pressed her foot as hard as she dared on the accelerator. She loved feeling the night air rush by, the wind in her hair. She loved the feeling of power—like the car was an extension of her own body, like *she* went right out of her arms through her hands into the steering wheel. Mind meld. Cyborg. One with a machine. She pushed harder on the pedal, 60, 70, 80, her foot stretching out, her heart pounding, her fingers clenching the wheel, 90. She got it up to one hundred. They were flying, really flying. The wind and the rain and the lights in the distance streaming by like a time-lapsed photograph. See, she remembered thinking, see. There's nothing to be afraid of. Her mother was afraid of everything and she wanted out of that box. If you were too careful, could you even call it living? Joshua thought the same way she did. He was always quoting things he'd read in books, like, *proximity to death brings proximity to life* and *if you live in fear of death, you're not really alive.* She knew he didn't have a death wish or anything; he wasn't like those guys at Columbine; he just thought of death as a kind of metaphor. For freedom. Freedom from fear.

After she had brought the car back down, they had pulled over on an exit and climbed out. It was so dark, the sky was reeling with stars. She walked off in the brush to pee, and he kept making rattlesnake sounds, throwing rocks over where she was squatting, trying not to get her pants wet and so, when he peed, standing in front of the car but just off to the side, she had put the headlights on him. They started laughing, still giddy from the speed, everything hysterically funny, the sky one with the desert and everything spinning around them, and so when they got back in, the laughing became kissing, this breathless kissing, their hands moving over each other, on top of the clothes, beneath the clothes. She wanted to feel his skin next to hers, his mouth on her, she wanted to touch him, feel her hands slide over his chest, across his shoulders, down his arms. And they kissed like that, tenderly, urgently, finally their shirts off, her breasts against his chest, their hands over each others' pants, moving, until they both came. And then, they sat. Kissing more quietly. Suddenly a little shy. Looking at each other. He ran his fingertips lightly over her breasts and she put her open palm over his heart. She could feel it. They were half naked together in the front seat of the car, in the moonlight, and it didn't even seem weird.

As she drove, Gloria found her mind drifting: studying in Florence again, gallery openings, a studio in Soho. All those dreams she'd had when she was in school—oh, she knew you were supposed to become an adult, give up on such fantasies, but she had never been able to give up completely. Instead, she had tried to live as an artist, see the world as an artist. When Danika was a baby and she'd had no time to work at all, she had arranged dishes in the drainer, just so, or hung clothes on the line, or endlessly rearranged objects on the mantle, telling herself, this is a still life. This, an altar. This, a domestic installation. It had been silly, of course, and she had still felt trapped. Worse, Danika had known. Even when she was little. Whenever Gloria complained, Danika would say things like, if it's that hard to be my mom, why did you even have me? Now that she was older, she had refined her methods of torture.

Not that Gloria needed help in the torture department—when she was putting the pieces in her portfolio, nothing pleased her, not even the work she considered finished. And she had just started the new work, inspired by a painting of Leonardo's she'd come across in the Uffizi all those years ago. She'd unearthed a print for her students and found herself in love all over again: a Madonna and Child in sepia with darker figures circling them. There were ghostly faces rising to the surface, even horses, where older layers of the painting were bleeding through, a staircase rising up, a building in the background, small figures like devils or tormented souls over on the left, faint scenes of an ancient battle over on the right, a palimpsest of the past. A record of his process. She loved it. And she loved the trees, Asian looking because of the dark ink, the bold stylized strokes seeming to float over the surface of the painting.

She was trying to get that same feeling, beginning sometimes with sepia washes or even sepia photographs, and then drawing with ink. Etchings over a wash or over watercolor. She had been experimenting with doing etchings in layers. Drypoint. More than one plate for the image, then ink over that. The process of carving with a needle into the copper or into the resin was more meticulous than the kind of work she liked to do but it had become a kind of meditation. Tedious at first and then liberating as she allowed herself to make mistakes, to incorporate them into the design and slip, like she always did, out of default, she knew, into a more abstract mode. She had always loved the not-knowing of the process. Not knowing what would happen when she layered images. Not knowing what another wash over an image would do to the ink, for instance. It could ruin it, maybe that was the thrill, but even the failures were more interesting to her than careful, deliberate pieces that seemed polished, technically good but somehow passionless. And she liked the layering, how it gave the piece a visual texture, how the work took on its own life, a life not dictated by her intentions.

She was afraid of showing this work, afraid, not of what the guy might say, but that seeing his face looking at it would somehow taint it. That image of his face would intervene. She liked working the way she did now. Without critics, without their voices in her head. Post-Danika, her work had become private. The masters had been exorcised. Maybe that's why the photo transfers had appealed to her—the serendipity of them. You could not go back and re-do or un-do anything. Their imperfections had to be accepted. That, and their size, made them intimate. Like a glimpse of a moment. Vivid and then gone. The etchings, that's what she liked about them, too, the scale. They were tiny. Smaller than snapshots. And she framed them in fairly large Plexiglas frames, with bolts at the corners, which made them seem modern, yet diaphanous. Transitory. As if they were suspended in a gelatinous light. That's what she was trying to capture, the feeling that each moment had layers of other moments beneath it, but was somehow still singular. Moments ticking by. Fragile as old film.

When they got to the mall, Danika did not want to go in, but what else was she supposed to do? She had been hoping for the big mall, with all the department stores, but this was a chi-chi mall in upscale Scottsdale. Full of equally chi-chi galleries, she was sure.

Her mom got out and smoothed her skirt down. Held her hands up to her hair, patting the back of it to make sure it wasn't falling out of the French twist. She looked at Danika—who thought she looked pale.

"Are you okay?"

"Do I look okay?"

Danika nodded. Her mom shut the door.

"Aren't you going to take your portfolio?" she asked her.

"I can always come back for it." Gloria shrugged. "If the guy even asks to see it."

Danika thought her mom looked like a kid. Scared. Young. Most of the time, she was so sure, so sure it was irritating, always impatient with Danika's doubts. How will you know unless you try? That's what she always said. Better to fail than to never even try.

"You look great, Mom," Danika put her arm around her. "Just tell me and I can come and get the portfolio, okay?"

Salima. Her mom's friend from art school. It was her opening and when she'd told her mom to send samples of work, Gloria had seemed excited and terrified in equal parts. Sure, she sold her photo transfers in cafés and gift shops around town, arranged art shows for the students in the Charter Art School where she taught, but Danika had never thought of her as a real artist. Salima, at the gallery, her black silk sheath, red slides, her peroxide hair as sleek as a cap; now Salima was obviously an artist. When she held her hands out, hammered silver bracelets dangled from both wrists. "Gloria," she gushed, grasping her hands and then hugging her, but her face was transparent, at least to Danika: Oh, Gloria. Poor dear. What's happened to you?

Even worse than suddenly seeing her mother through Salima's eyes, Danika thought, was the fact that she agreed with her. At home, in the sandwich shop, her mom had looked fine, sophisticated, even. The short skirt and sleeveless linen blouse with the mandarin collar were both modern, pretty fashionable, not like the stuff she wore to work. After all, Danika had picked them both out. The blouse was jade green, a few shades lighter than the skirt. And the French twist was not bad; her mom had fastened it with these things that looked like fancy chopsticks. "Très chic, no?" she had said to Danika as she applied some mascara and lipstick before they left the parking lot of the sandwich shop. Her mother never wore lipstick. Twice, before they even got on the freeway, she told Danika that Salima had promised to give her some advice on promoting her work.

But when Danika saw through Salima's eyes, she noticed that her mom's linen skirt and blouse had become hopelessly wrinkled on the two-hour drive, her hair was beginning to escape the French twist in large loopy strands. She didn't belong with these people, all of whom seemed fake, like they had stepped out of some fashion magazine. Danika loved the work her mom did, some of the Polaroid transfers were awesome, but she was glad she'd left them in the car. Salima wouldn't be impressed.

Danika wished they could both disappear. In fact, she did disappear. She made a quick exit from the gallery and sat outside on a bench in the mall and watched through the window. At first, her mom was laughing and talking to Salima and the other glossy women who were rushing around doing last-minute things, and then, for a while, she disappeared and then, when she reappeared, she was talking to this tall man. He had dark curly hair. Kinda like Danika's dad. Which made her stomach hurt. Was it him? By the way her mom tilted her head when she laughed, by the way her hands kept straying up to her hair, Danika could tell she liked him. But there was some kind of strain, too, her eyes looked tired. Fatigue was pulling on the corners of her mouth. She looked like she wanted to cry. So it *was* him. Which made Danika feel like crying. Her mom suddenly reminded her of the unpopular girl in school, the brainy one who always tried too hard. Her hair was escaping in ever larger strands and she kept trying to tuck it back in. When she raised her arms, Danika saw dark rings on the new linen blouse; she hated sweat stains, but at least her mom had shaved her pits. Sometimes she forgot and the scraggly hairs made Danika feel as if her mother were exposing her private parts.

Dan studied the huge Cubist painting of a woman's face just behind her mother and the man she was sure was her father. Why did he even matter? That's what she couldn't figure out. She didn't miss him. In fact, when she was little, she'd thought he was some visiting relative. Like her grandmother. Somebody who had popped in once or twice with presents and who sent cards at the right times of year although, always, a few days late. As if he could never ever remember the exact date of anything. Not even Christmas. Certainly not her birthday.

She squinted. Why had they even come? This was not her idea of art. The colors were garish, the mouths leering, the paint globby and shiny as if it were still wet. Art was supposed to open something up inside you, not make you want to look away. Most of Salima's paintings were of girls and women, none were beautiful, some were very ugly. Some were just parts of a woman's body, a muscular thigh, say, a conical yet dimpled breast. In all of them, shards of colored glass were embedded in the paint; sometimes they protruded from the flesh like the heads of futuristic arrows.

Danika snorted a laugh. Here she had insisted on coming because she was afraid her mom would need her, for moral support. She always got so depressed if someone rejected her work. And now this: a drama that was sure to have a tragic ending.

When Gloria first saw Salima in the gallery, she'd felt immediately out of place. Provincial. Sweet. Other artists had always seemed polished to her, perfected facsimiles, neuroses so openly on display you had to wonder if there was any pain involved at all. She was being bitchy and she knew it, but this was a time warp for sure. They were the tragically hip and she was jealous. This was the life she had wanted.

The curator was an unassuming man. Not slick, not an ex-pat New Yorker—she always thought of people from the East, who settled in the West, as expatriates, somehow, from another infinitely more interesting country. No, he had the air of an old humanities professor, which made Gloria like him immediately. She liked the fact that he was wearing a blue checked shirt. One of his fingernails looked as if it had been smashed with a hammer and she found this endearing. He had direct blue eyes. They sat in a back room and he asked her how long it had been since she was in school with Salima.

Gloria had to think about it. Danika was seventeen. "Seventeen," she said. Seventeen years. "No, eighteen," she said. She had to count the pregnancy. She'd forgotten about that—which caused, suddenly, this overwhelming sense of time, that it had passed her by. She didn't want to say, teaching, she'd been teaching, raising a child, because, after all, didn't that seem like an excuse? Didn't other artists have lives, too? And didn't they have something to show for all those years?

He spread the work she'd sent him out on the table in front of them. Of course, it was the older work he liked better. The abstracts of the desert she'd been doing several years ago. It was more focused, he said. More polished. Clearer as far as intent.

Then he held his hand over one of the newer pieces, circling first over one part and then over another. "This image," he said, "is, well, evocative but somehow... amorphous. Where do you want my eye to go?"

It was such a basic question. She should have seen it for herself. These images were all in a private language. She suddenly felt like he was her favorite professor, the one who'd wanted her to do well, but who had clearly despaired of her ever being able to pull it off.

"It's hard to sell abstract work in this market," he sighed. "People out here still think of photos as representational. And tourists want Southwestern. You know, missions. Landscape. Ansel Adams. Or Curtis, sepia Indians."

She was glad she'd left her latest work in the car. If he thought these were unfocused, abstract, what would he think of the etchings? But going back to images like the photos would be almost as bad as doing perpetual photo transfers of purple prickly pear and blue doors. What was it about blue doors, anyway? Why did everyone love blue doors? Blue doors in Provençe, in Capri, in Mexico, even in Istanbul for Christ's sake. What about red doors? She had this image of herself running into poster shops in the malls; she would grab posters of blue doors and tear them to shreds. One after another. She would be arrested. Hospitalized. Doctors would search for a medication that could erase the color blue from her mind.

"Send more," he said. "Whenever you're ready. I would be glad to see anything you have."

He rose and she rose and that was the end of it.

And now she had to go out into the gallery and smile and look interested in Salima's work, which had always been too flashy for her taste, the strokes way too broad, without complication. Salima's paintings, she had always thought, were in billboard language. They shouted. They broadcast. Frankly, they were boring.

There she was, being bitchy again.

And there he was.

Nick in the flesh. Wouldn't you know it? Add insult to injury. Nick. Standing next to the skinniest, most punctured—even her nipples, clearly visible beneath the nearly transparent and entirely too small baby tee shirt, were pierced—platinum blonde. Black roots. Ghoulish eye shadow *around* her eyes. Part heroin-chic fashion model, part Cindy Sherman self-portrait. Scary.

Gloria wanted to drag Danika into the room. See! she would whisper furiously into her ear, see what I'm afraid of!? See what happens to girls who don't graduate from high school! But she knew it probably wasn't true. This girl was probably a successful artist—or by the looks of her tortured body, one of Salima's models.

Nick had better not be dating her.

But Miss Punctured Waif was the next person going in to talk to the curator—evidently, he was willing to meet with almost anyone—and Nick had been waiting to see her. Gloria. And so, rock in her stomach, she had gone on automatic: she smiled, she laughed, she cocked her head as if she were listening when all the while there was a roaring fire inside her.

Right when Danika decided no one would notice and started to light up, the man who was her father appeared—or, as she sometimes thought of him now, the man who had fathered her. That was more accurate. To think she had once been obsessed with having a dad! Her mom's boyfriend Marcus didn't count, of course. For one, he didn't live with them; for two, the only dad-things he ever did were teach her how to dribble a soccer ball and pound a few nails in the house whenever it was falling apart. She had always thought she missed having a dad but then, one day, she was ten, it was her birthday, Nick had shown up, late, of course, and stayed for all of one hour and she realized: she didn't miss *him*. She didn't have any actual memories of him. Nick. Whatever she had thought were memories had always been pictures: she could never visualize him in motion, for instance, outside of those pictures, and the words of the memories were her mother's, so it was like the memories had been implanted in her but weren't *hers* and so, if she didn't have any actual memories, how could she miss *him*?

Up close, gray in his dark hair.

"Aren't you too young to smoke?" he asked her.

She forced herself to look only at the lit match, not him. She shrugged. She wanted to be nonchalant. "Legally." She exhaled a stream of smoke. "I don't see any cops."

He sat down next to her. "Got an extra light?"

She handed him the matchbook.

"Nasty habit," he said.

"Spare me."

After a while, after about half a cigarette, more precisely, he said, "So you do remember me."

When she looked at his profile, her stomach hurt. She wanted to lean her head against his shoulder. She wanted him to put his arm around her as if it were the most natural gesture in the world. Damn. Maybe she had PMS.

He was studying her face. "I'd like to get to know you," he said.

"Not like there's a rush."

"Touché."

Touché ? She rolled her eyes. How cheesy was that?

"Better late than never," she said. "At least that's what I've heard."

She looked up at the gallery through the window. She couldn't see her mother anywhere. Did she know he was out here? Had she known he would be here? Where *was* she?

Gloria splashed water on her face in the bathroom. Why hadn't it occurred to her that he might be here? How could Salima have neglected to tell her? She needed time to compose herself. She looked at herself in the mirror again. What *had* she agreed to? Dinner next week so he could "get to know" Danika? Was it possible she had agreed to that? She groaned. What else? Did she really think she'd let Dan *fly* to stay with him for part of the summer? God, she hoped Danika wouldn't want to. A week without her seemed, suddenly, not delicious, not a luxury, but empty. And Dan on a plane? By herself? Terrifying.

She took the chopsticks out of her hair and shook it out. Why did it have to be so unruly? She combed water through it, smoothed it back into a ponytail, which she fastened at the nape of her neck. She couldn't believe how her heart had constricted when she saw him. How she could feel her body move beneath her clothes, her breasts brushing against the fabric of her blouse. Her nipples. The silk of her slip against her inner thighs. She had even been acutely aware of her underwear. God. She was sure she'd had a ridiculous smile on her face when she was talking to him. Tell her she hadn't been that transparent.

He had always been hard to resist, amazing in his own way, the way he saw the shapes and structures of the world, the way he loved color, could talk about artists and movies and philosophy. There was something seductive about someone who was as good as he was. His paintings opened something in her, in her heart, her eyes; even now she sometimes found herself hungry for them. And then, the first time they'd gone up to his apartment and opened a bottle of wine, he'd looked directly into her eyes as he unbuttoned her blouse. She remembered that. Always. The way he could read her. The rough texture of his fingertips on her skin.

Finally, though, it was his moods. She couldn't bear them. He'd spend days doing nothing but drinking; she'd wake up in the morning to see him slumped in a chair watching her, a half-empty bottle of Cuervo in his hand. He was always sorry, he didn't know what got into him, she was everything, he'd make it up to her. Okay. But how could she bring a child into that?

"Your mother," Nick said, "was doing remarkable work."

Danika looked at him. He was serious. And shouldn't he know? She had seen his paintings in a book. So her mother could have been an artist? She could have chosen a different life? Danika had always thought that adults simply had the lives they had. It had never occurred to her that each person had several *possible* lives.

"She's got her portfolio in the car," Danika said, dangling the keys in front of him.

"She might not like it, for me to see them. Without her permission."

"Like I've never pissed her off before."

When he laughed, Danika felt like she was conspiring with him. She could feel her heart getting both warm and scared. He would just leave again. That much was for sure. She might never see him again. This might be it.

Seize the day.

Wasn't that what her mom said? So how could she get *too* mad?

She dangled the keys again, like music. Her mother was still nowhere in sight and so they snuck out into the blistering twilight and sat in the car, AC on, and looked through her mother's portfolio. Danika had opened it, expecting to see the stuff she took around to the cafés and shops in town: photo transfers, photographs of the desert, some hand tinted, but instead, there were collages. Fragments of photos, paint, handwriting. Some of them were very small. Even the larger ones were only the size of a postcard. There were also black-and-white etchings: eerie, indistinct figures trailed across darkness, lights were blurs of white or thin lines of silver. The images caught at Danika's breath, reminded her of dreams.

"You can see it here," Nick said quietly, "a kind of integrity. Even in school, when the rest of us were so anxious to please the professors, she would never show anything until she was sure it was ready."

He flipped back and looked at the etchings again. "Here," he said, "and here. You can really see it."

"It's been hard for her," Danika said, realizing suddenly that it had been. "Are you going to help her?"

"I can try."

"Do you really want to get to know me?"

"Yeah," he said, nodding his head, "I do."

But how was that supposed to happen, Danika wondered. Chance meetings every seven years?

"I'd give you my card," she said, "if I had one."

He looked up from the portfolio, surprised, and laughed. "I remember where you live."

"Yeah, all of the women in Salima's paintings looked wounded," Danika agreed with her mom on the drive home. That was obvious. "But *none* of them had hair in their pits," she pointed out.

"Well," Gloria said, "I just don't get it."

"What?" Danika asked, "that it's gross?"

"No," she sighed, "conceptual art. When the explanation is more interesting than the work itself."

If Danika hated one thing about her mother, this was it: she never talked about the real thing. No. Here she was, talking about conceptual art. Like Danika gave a shit. She wanted to talk about Nick. Ask questions. Get some answers. What had he meant, for instance, by saying he remembered where they lived?

She had been sitting on the bench with him again when her mom had reappeared in the gallery. She had slicked her hair down with water and made a little bun on the back of her neck. She really looked like a teacher, in other words. Worse. She had her glasses on. She looked like a TV version of a librarian. What a dork her mother was. First she had been acting all flirty with him and now it seemed like she wanted to scare him away. After she said something to Salima, she walked out the door and saw Danika sitting on the bench; she saw her sitting with Nick, but she didn't even go over. She just motioned for Danika to follow her. A little wave of her hand to him. "Good to see you again," she had called, and started walking toward the outside doors.

Danika had no choice but to mimic her. She stood up, opened and shut her hand in a quick flutter. "Good to see you again," she chirped.

Okay, it had been a cheap shot. She knew that. She had made him laugh—but at Gloria's expense. Still. Couldn't her mom even sit and talk for a few minutes? First time she sees her dad in seven years and her mom can't even ask him out for a drink? What was she afraid of? That Marcos would get jealous?

"In school," her mother was saying, "that's how it was. They all wanted me to make some sort of statement. Expected me to incorporate *la virgen de Guadalupe* into my work. Or *la llorona*. An homage to Frida. Just because I'm Mexican. Or, you know, make some feminist comment… photograph fat girls or something."

"That's what Nick said," Danika studied her profile. "That you did what you wanted."

"Hhmmm?" Her mother made a surprised sound and turned to look at Danika for a minute. "You're lucky you don't have his nose," she smiled.

"Why didn't you tell me he was going to be there?"

"I didn't know." Gloria looked back at the road. Her hands tightened on the wheel. "What did you want me to do?" She paused. "I was supposed to be *happy* to see him?"

"God, Mom. I just asked."

She sighed. "Sorry."

"Sorry? Remember that when I say it."

Gloria reached out and took Danika's hand. Even though she tried to pull it away, Gloria held on. There was a whole story she couldn't tell her daughter. Not how she'd felt trapped. What? She was supposed to become her mother? Married to some drunk? To a man who would never be faithful? Plus, he hadn't exactly protested when she broke it off. Especially once she told him she was pregnant. *Tie the noose around my neck* was basically how he'd felt about it.

Neither could she tell Danika about the abortion clinic. Obviously she hadn't been able to go through with it, but she didn't want Dan to know that deciding to have her had been the worst day of her life. She'd sat in the car—her however-lapsed Catholicism kept her from even opening the door—trying to breathe through the choked feeling in her throat. She couldn't breathe. She couldn't even get enough breath to cry. Her choices stopped here. Her life would never have that open-endedness of youth again. No more studying in Florence. No studio in New York. No more thinking about what *she* wanted, period. And what the hell was she going to do? She was twenty-two years old, had exactly four thousand dollars, no job, a for-practical-purposes worthless B.F.A.—the first woman in her family to go to college and she had quixotically majored in art—and the baby would arrive in seven months.

"I didn't make it easy for him, Dan. Okay? Guilty as charged."

"He could have done anything he wanted."

"True." He was a trust-fund baby, he could've done a hell of a lot more—but she didn't want Danika to judge him, not like she had judged her dad, so she softened her voice, "At least he helped support you. Hey, if he doesn't spend it all, you could be rich someday."

"Ooooh. Money," she snorted a laugh. "Guilt money."

Danika knew her mother still loved Nick. She knew because she could hear the fear in her mom's voice. But how she felt about Nick didn't have anything to do with Marcos—which was exactly how Danika felt about Joshua and Abbie. She thought maybe she loved Joshua but that afternoon, at the party at his house, she'd been lying on his bed with Abbie and when Josh went down to the bar in the basement, where everyone else was, to get more vodka, Abbie had started kissing her and Danika hadn't told her to stop. She had closed her eyes and let Abbie kiss her and it was the same feeling as kissing Josh. And then Abbie was running her hand up under her blouse and Danika had let her. Because she was curious. She wanted Abbie to touch her and all inside, it was like heat, like light, and she was afraid. Her heart pounding, she had told Abbie to stop. She'd told her don't, I can't do this, and Abbie had just smiled like she knew something Danika didn't know.

Later, with Josh, she closed her eyes and they had kissed and she had let him undress her and the whole time, she was wondering if she was doing this because she'd been drinking, or because she wanted to, or because she wanted to prove to herself that she wanted Josh more than she wanted Abbie. His skin was smooth, he was kissing her and she felt the same fire, her heart pounding, his mouth on her breast, is it okay? Pushing against her, is it okay? She felt him push inside her. And that was scary, too, how something hot had opened up inside her, then all her feeling, it seemed, was concentrated right there, then the pulsing moving through her in waves. And then that was over and she felt naked, felt his breath on her neck, felt his fingertips running up and down her sides, felt his mouth on her in all the places that kissing had made come alive.

She supposed that was the kind of thing you could *never* tell your father.

"I'm not a virgin any more," she announced.

Her mom was quiet, for a long time it seemed. Just the sound of the tires on the still sticky asphalt. The eighteen wheelers, when they whizzed by, sucked the air from around the car.

"What kind of name is Joshua for a Mexican anyways?" her mother snapped.

"His mom's white."

"Oh."

"I just told you I had sex!"

"I know!" She snapped again. "Did you use a condom at least?"

"God. You don't have to get mad. It's not like you never did it."

"Did he use a condom?" Gloria repeated in a deliberate voice.

Danika shrugged. "He said he would."

"Well, did it feel all rubbery?"

"God, Mom, I didn't touch it."

"God, Danika, if you can't touch it, it doesn't have any business inside of you."

"Right. You always practiced safe sex."

Sometimes Danika wondered why she tried to tell her mother anything. She cracked the window and lit a cigarette. She guessed smoking was the least of her mom's worries now.

"So why did you do it?" Gloria finally asked.

"Why did you?"

Her mother looked at her and raised an eyebrow and Danika knew the offense-as-defense tactic wasn't going to work.

"I asked you first."

"Because we wanted to."

"Did he pressure you?"

"No. I wanted to as much as he did."

Gloria held her hand out and Danika put the lit cigarette between her fingers.

"Can you trust him?"

"I think so," Danika shrugged. "I thought you loved Marcos."

"Of course I do." Gloria took a couple of big hits. "Man," she exhaled, "it has been one of those days." She shook her head. "One of those fricking days."

"But you still love Nick."

"Well, I'm attracted to him," her mom started laughing, "Damn, am I attracted to him. Goddamn."

"My lips are sealed," Danika said, suddenly contemplating an entirely different future.

Gloria pulled the car over on an exit. She finished smoking Danika's cigarette. She was trying to figure out what to say. All of Dan's life, she had been planning these two moments: telling her the truth about her dad, saying the right thing if Dan told her she'd had sex. She had failed on both counts. She had drawn a complete blank.

She looked at her daughter. The night was gray behind her. She needed to tell her that virginity was not all it was cracked up to be. Losing it didn't change her. Just because you had sex once didn't mean you had to have it again. She needed to tell her that fertilizing an egg didn't make a man a father. Actually, she wasn't sure she needed to say any of this, but it was hard to see Danika's eyes. She took her face in the palms of her hands.

"I did the right thing," she said. "He was a drinker. He was depressed all the time." She kissed Dan's forehead. "He would have made us miserable."

"I kind of want to get to know him, anyways."

Gloria sighed. "Oh, Dani. Oh, *mi'ja*." She leaned her cheek against the headrest and closed her eyes. "I know."

She sighed again. Saw, for some reason, the rumpled sheets in her bed, the bed she had shared with Marcos, at least on weekends, for the past thirteen years. The photographs she'd hung on the living room walls. Her dishes on the open shelves Marcos had built in the kitchen. The artifacts of her life, a life she had carefully arranged. Marcos was a funny and tender man. Danika was as honest and smart as she was willful. Teaching was a good enough job. And now, now Dan was nearly grown, she finally had time to do her own work—but was that enough? Why did she suddenly want more? Why did she want to be the girl she had been, the girl who took risks? Why did safe, balanced, sane feel like a trap? After all, if she had been someone who played it safe, Danika would never have been born. And here she was, Danika, Dan, Dani, the heart around which everything else cohered.

"I almost had sex with a girl," Danika said.

Gloria was so surprised that she heard herself laugh, a quick, *huh?*

"I mean," Danika quickly clarified. "Josh left for a while. And then this girl kissed me. And then he came back."

They were both quiet, it seemed like a long time. Gloria wasn't sure what to say. It sounded a little complicated.

"Do you like girls better?"

Danika just shrugged.

"Well," Gloria said slowly, as if she were measuring the words, "it's easy to love two people." She shook her head. "But, probably, you shouldn't sleep with both of them."

"You think?" Danika laughed.

It was Gloria's turn to shrug. "Not at the same time, well." She wanted another cigarette. Hell, she wanted a drink.

"Maybe I should drive," Danika said.

When they got out of the car to change places, the air was still hot. The sky looked like a dark ocean, full of waves made silver by a moon that was nowhere in sight.

not a matter of love

DRI

There was a platter with a slab of London broil, medium rare, a bowl of fresh green beans, and a salad of sliced beefsteak tomatoes and dilled cucumber. Plate silver, not the sterling. The everyday china. Jackie's stepfather was taking the bull by the horns. He wanted to know what had happened to his rum.

This is what: it was last Tuesday, high noon when Jackie woke up. Still three hours before her stepsister Lisa would be home from junior high—Jackie wished she liked Lisa, she tried to like her, but there was something so cheerleader about her—so she poured herself a rum and coke to pass the time and stole a cigarette out of the pack her mother kept hidden in the kitchen. Looking out at the pool, at the grass gone to weeds under the grape arbor, she remembered the first time she and Walker had done it. It had been there, under the arbor at midnight. Nothing romantic about it. The dried grass sticking her in the butt and back. She had changed her mind, said no, but he had kept on. It hurt. She held her breath and studied the light in the pool, its round eye blinking behind murky waves, a moon in water.

On the afternoon of stolen rum, Jackie had decided to read the journal she'd kept in high school and so took the bottle with her out to the back porch. As she leafed through, even the most innocuous entries were like Golden Oldies. Or smelling a certain scent. Orange blossoms and there she is, sixteen, in the elementary schoolyard halfway between Walker's house and hers. They've just finished pushing each other on the swings and she's leaning up against the rough brick building. He takes a hit off the joint, blows the smoke in her face, teasing, takes another hit, the pot crackling, leans over her, his thin blond hair falling forward, *ready?* he says, *shotgun*, another stream of smoke, his hand on the wall behind her. There's a slice of a pale moon in the sky above his head. He leans forward, his lips brush hers ever so lightly. This must be love.

He has her cornered in her mother's kitchen, her bare back sticking to the bleached mahogany cabinets, he leans into her, the tip of his tongue between his white teeth, his thigh presses between her legs, his fingers play up under her bikini top, his finger playing right there, right there, a surge of heat from her nipple to her crotch, his face against her throat. Her mother's voice from the patio, the scraping of the screen door. Move it, Walker, your hand. He grins, no, make me, laughing. She pushes him away, fear rushing to her face, making it hot. Her mother looks at them. She knows. Turns, gets a beer from the refrigerator, and leaves.

A ritual burning, that was the way to deal with the past. Jackie switched to shots and smoked her mother's cigarettes and lit match after match, setting each piece of paper on fire, watching the flame, watching the ink become metallic, the paper blacken and curl. Burning those words felt like the rum going down: pure burn and then the space opening up in her head.

But all three of them—Paul, Jackie's mother, Lisa—were waiting, forks poised mid-air, for her answer.

Jackie shrugged, "You want me to pay you back?"

"Damn straight," he said cutting his meat. Then he looked up, "And no drinking when you're supposed to be here for Lisa."

"I know that."

He kept up his stern look, Old Eagle Eyes, she secretly called it. He waited.

"I drank before she got home from school."

"And if there'd been an emergency?"

"There wasn't."

He narrowed his eyes again. Do you get the point? You are eighteen now, Miss Missy. No such thing as free rent. Not in this life. But he didn't have to say it. That was how it had been from day one. The minute he moved in, his calculator started adding up each bite she took.

"Did I drive anywhere?" she asked Lisa.

Lisa shook her head a vigorous no.

"Was I drunk?"

Like Alice in Wonderland, Lisa had long blonde hair and a long bland face and she was waiting for something surprising to happen. Until then, she'd be overly cheerful. She wanted Jackie to like her. She didn't like Jackie but she did like the idea of a cool big sister. It gave her currency with the popular kids.

"No," Lisa said, looking down at her plate, sneaking sideways glances at both her father and Jackie, trying to decide who it was more important to please, "no. We couldn't tell at all."

And then she added (to make herself credible? Jackie wondered, or because she really hated the nasty habit, as she called it, wrinkling her rabbit nose), "We could tell you'd been smoking cigarettes, though."

Jackie has one memory that, for her, defines everything. She walks out onto the back porch and there, sitting on the lawn furniture, are her mother and stepdad and Lisa. They are reminiscing. Jackie pulls up a fourth chair but they don't notice her. Paul is telling her mother about Lisa's childhood, the time she flooded the neighbor's basement with a garden hose, the time she ran away on her tricycle, only three years old, so daring! the time she won the tap dancing contest, cute as a button! not shy at all!—and Jackie says, remember the time we went to the San Francisco Zoo?

Her mother looks at her with a puzzled expression, says, we never went to the San Francisco Zoo.

Jackie begins to say, then where did we see the baboon? but Paul interrupts, says, Lisa had personality, was always into mischief, but you, he shakes his head and chuckles, I bet you were a crybaby.

Jackie knows what Paul really wants to say: your father left, I took his place. Get over it.

She is her father's daughter, her mother says, shaking her smooth blonde head, adding up all of Jackie's father's sins, so sorrowful. Her mother always played the martyr, but Jackie had seen how her barbed remarks got caught in her father's flesh.

But Mom, Jackie says...

Jackie's mother has the photo album open on her lap. It's true, she says, there's a picture of everyone at our wedding except Jackie! What happened? There must be some missing.

Jackie takes the book from her mother. She's sure it's a mistake. She remembers being called up for the pictures, resenting it like hell, resenting being told to smile, resenting the dumb pink ruffled dress that her mother and Lisa had picked out because she had refused to go along. She remembers every small annoyance. The women from her mother's work, their lacquered hair, how they kept saying Paul was such a dear—it was about time Louise got lucky. As if Jackie's father were a complete loser. Which he was not. She remembers catching a glimpse of herself in a mirror: she was standing next to her mother, she was fourteen and she looked like a big, giant, clumsy, ugly girl-version of her mother who was so petite, so slim, so *au courant*. Beautiful. (Like Jackie Onassis, after whom her mother had named her but, of course, since the universe was nothing if not ironic, Jackie had blue eyes, frizzy white girl hair, and not one sophisticated bone in her body.) She remembers her older brother Greg sneaking off with the other boys to drink beers and smoke cigarettes. She wanted to follow him, but he told her to bug off, like she was as stupid as Lisa, like she and Lisa somehow inhabited the same category, even though she was almost as old as him and Lisa was only nine. She had wanted to sneak off and call her father, but she knew exactly what his voice would conjure: hair mussed, shirt unbuttoned, glass of scotch in his hand. She would hear, in the slur of his words, how many drinks he'd had, and if he weren't already drinking, the phone call would be sure to set him off.

She remembers looking at the photo album again. She can't find one picture of herself at the wedding. There, Paul and her mother are gazing at one another like cheesy teenagers. Lisa is beaming, and why not? The ruffled pink dress looks cute on her. Greg, at eighteen, is taller than Paul and looks like one of those cold Greek statues, the big nose, the blank eyes that see nothing, the curly hair. But no pictures of Jackie.

Did you throw them out? Jackie asks her mother.

It's so odd, her mother muses. What could have happened to them?

You threw your pictures out, Lisa says, don't you remember? That night you got so mad?

But Jackie doesn't remember. Oh, she remembers hating the pictures, but she can't imagine she tore them up. Is there something wrong with her memory? Why does she always remember everything different? Wrong?

You're just too sensitive, Paul says. It's your attitude. Remember, someone is always worse off than you.

Of course, when they were first married and Jackie had complained about Paul, her mother had tried to cajole her: you do want a car when you turn sixteen, don't you? Then, when Jackie asked why Paul was the Grand Pooh-Pah and got to have the Last Word in the house *her* father had built, it had unleashed in her mother such a torrent of bitterness that she never asked anything like that again. The tone of her mother's voice, pure anger and grief at the way life had betrayed her, cut deeper than the words. She believed her version of life was The Truth: I have put you first for years. I suffered with your father to put a roof over your head. It's time I think of my own happiness. Jackie had rolled her eyes. Please. You're becoming a cliché, she told her. Her mother's hand flew up, as if to slap her, but she stopped mid-air, stunned. Then the sound of her heels clicked across the tile floor in accusation.

"Oh!" her mother said, smiling brightly, "Frank, you remember? Janice's son? He wanted to know if you'd like to go out on Friday."

"Frank?" Jackie asked. "Oh. Frank. He reminds me of a golf pro."

Her mother tilted her head. "What's wrong with a golf pro?"

"Mom, he's what? Twenty-five? He doesn't want to go out with me."

"Oh, yes, he does. He said you were cute. Remember," she raised her eyebrows first at Jackie and then at Lisa, "it's just as easy to fall in love with a rich man as a poor man."

One night it was: if you go out with a Mexican boy, nice white boys won't be interested in you. Jackie knew her mother didn't say these things out of prejudice, not really, she wasn't even being mean-hearted. It was just, from her observation of the world, having grown up near a large Portuguese community, these things were simply true. People wouldn't accept you. Once you crossed the line, you didn't come back.

"Well," Jackie told her, "I've decided I don't like guys with blond hair. They want only one thing."

Dismay on her mother's face, Jackie had hurt her again. Maybe her mom was just trying to change the subject, protect her from one of Paul's tirades—which was next on the menu, they could all feel it—but Frank? The golf pro in the little red Triumph? If not for that car, he would be completely forgettable. And what did her mother think? That she had a tennis outfit hidden in her closet? God, her mother didn't have a clue. Why did she want so badly for Jackie to be someone else?

"I'm going down to Armando's tonight, anyway, and see what he's been doing."

All three of them, even Lisa, stopped eating and looked at her. Paul cleared his throat and said something about her mother not wanting her to drive down there at night, in that part of town.

"I work in that part of town. No different from any other part of town."

"Oh, yes it is," her mother said, "and you know it."

Paul said, "Why don't you just call him and have him come and pick you up? That's how it's supposed to work—anyway, how it did when I was young."

"Well," Jackie said, scooting back her chair, "times have changed."

Lisa said, "If Armando still likes you, how come he hasn't called? I mean, he hasn't even called. I wouldn't go crawling to him if I were you."

"What the hell do you know about anything?"

"Don't swear at your sister," Paul said.

"Then tell her to stay the hell out of it."

Louise shook her head and said quietly, "He doesn't love you. He just wants to use you."

"Look," Jackie said, trying to keep her voice calm, "don't tell me how he feels. You don't have any right to tell me how he feels."

It wasn't a matter of love, she wanted to tell her mother, it was a matter of living in her own skin. She liked the way his eyes fastened on hers when she talked to him, the way he bit his lower lip when he was learning new chords on the guitar. The way his dark hair fell over his eyes. His passion, period. He couldn't watch the evening news without erupting in anger. Once, as they walked down narrow city streets to a restaurant, they ran into a protest in front of the courthouse. Serendipity, he said, Support your local Sanctuary Movement! So they each waved a sign at the passing cars. It had seemed romantic. There was a full moon. He put his face next to hers so they could see from the same perspective. In Mexico, he said, they see a rabbit in the moon. Once, he showed her how to make tortillas. (Hers all looked like amoebas.) Once, when they were making love, he stopped and pulled a book out from under the bed. Pretended to look something up. Oh, he'd said, *that's* how you do it! She'd laughed. She'd never known it was okay to laugh while you were making love. He was nothing like Walker.

"You are only doing this as an act of rebellion. Something to get back at me," her mother said, cutting her steak furiously. "Well, I'm not going to feed your rebellion. Go out with him, if you want to, invite him for dinner. Let him see how we live. Then, if he loves you, he will leave you alone because he'll see he's not right for you."

And so, even though the world had gone on, her mother still believed there were outward signs, whether you ate with sterling or plate silver or stainless steel, where you lived, went to school, what kind of work you did, how you dressed, the color of your skin. These outward signs were what mattered to her. And yet outward signs deceived.

Paul cleared his throat. "All your mother means is if he cared for you at all, he wouldn't want you driving around alone at night."

"That is *not* what I meant." Louise gave him a sharp look and then looked at Jackie. "A man like that wants only one thing from a girl like you. He's taking advantage of your innocence."

"Mother," Jackie laughed, "I am not innocent. I haven't been for a long time."

Paul's face turned red; he told Lisa to leave the table.

"He doesn't love you," Louise said.

Jackie said nothing. She stood up and took her dishes to the sink. She had always tried to be quiet, had always tried to acquiesce to everything, at least at home—of course, she did whatever she wanted behind their backs and then lied, as necessary. Lied to preserve her *mother's* innocence. To keep the peace.

Jackie, her mother had said once, you've built a wall around yourself. I can't get in. But Jackie knew she didn't want in. She didn't want to hear the truth. She never had.

Just for instance: when Jackie tried to tell her that Paul had come into her bedroom late one night (obviously drunk, in his underwear, she woke up to him sitting on her bed, saying, I know you think I'm the bad guy here... we can't force you to be a part of this family... what makes you think you're so special?), her mother had been playing the piano. Jackie sat down next to her. She wanted to tell her about Paul's anger, about the underwear, about his drink sloshing on her bed—the threat, his being there in her room was a threat, and he was doing it deliberately, and it had scared her. Her mother stopped playing and looked at her like, yes, and Jackie had opened her mouth and her mother had said, yes? Jackie's face was hot. She sat there, her mouth opening and closing, like she was a goldfish. She put one finger on a white key; the note rang clear as a bell. Paul, she whispered. Her mother had sighed:

can't this wait?

It had never happened again, but after that she always knew what was beneath his smile, his measured words. She knew he was marking time until she left. She knew the only way to be close to her mother was to hurt her. In a way, it wasn't fair to blame her mother, but she did. She blamed her. Not for Paul, exactly, not even for the rift he had caused between them, but for the way Jackie had to keep everything inside. The way she had to absorb pain because her mother was too fragile.

And, although it was equally unfair, she blamed her mother for Walker. For the way she needed him. Or, maybe, more accurately, for the way she needed to please him.

For this: Jackie had let him take a picture of her nude. He had a Polaroid Instamatic and so, he argued, no one would ever see it but him. She was curious and he was persistent, and so she let him take a picture of her topless, but when she saw the picture, it frightened her. She told him he had to destroy it, and he'd said, couldn't we just cut your head off? And he took the scissors and cut her head off and there she was, just a torso. No, she told him, no. But I want to keep it, he said, to remember you by, in case you leave me, and he started cutting in a spiral, around and around until only one breast was left. Can't I keep this? he asked. She took it and flushed it down the toilet. She tore the black paper negative into small pieces, watched them swirl down the toilet. She felt sick—and all because she had seen, on a small circle of paper, her breast and the look on his face as he held it in his hand.

After she broke up with him, he haunted the shop where she worked. One day, she was talking to a customer, laughing, and there was Walker. After the guy left, Walker followed her into the back room. If I ever see you talking to him again... He cornered her near the window. He touched her face. You like him. I can tell. The way you look at him... his mouth was close to hers. She hoped the manager would come back from lunch soon. Walker, she said. The bell on the front door chimed. Walker, she said again. They could hear the customer calling out. You have to come back, Jackie, or I'll... he kissed her mouth hard, his teeth on her closed lips, I'll... his finger drifted down to the neckline of her tee shirt, I'll... the threat scarier, in a way, because it was so vague, unfinished, could mean anything. He was running his fingertip back and forth along the neckline, his nail barely brushing her throat. I'm sorry, his face collapsing. Why do you get me like this? Why do you do this to me?

But her mother had liked Walker. Of course. He was from a good family, had a scholarship. He was smooth and charming and got his manners growing up in Dallas, where they still said *pardon?* and ma'am and yes, sir! and nigger.

After she did the dinner dishes, Jackie walked down to her room. Her mother followed, stood in the doorway and watched her. It was going to rain, you could smell rain through the open window. The pyracantha branches were tapping against the screen. Jackie started throwing her things into boxes.

Her mother said, calmly, "Take only what you can carry."

She'd said this before, when Jackie was little and threatened to run away. Take the clothes you're wearing and don't come back. It had always stopped her before. But this time Jackie didn't care if she never came back.

Her mother tried again, "You make your bed, you'll have to lie in it." She could be stern, she believed in consequences. But once, she had told Jackie that she hated to think about her in that part of town. What if you get sick or you need me, she had asked. You may as well be in another country, she'd said.

Jackie looked at her mother, and it was killing her, the sorrow on her face. She wished it could be like when she was little and her mother had held her, made her feel safe and loved, but now she just felt trapped.

She kept packing. Lisa was standing in the doorway. "I'm sorry," she said.

Jackie looked at her. "This isn't your fault." She studied Lisa's face, softened her voice so Lisa would believe her. "This doesn't have anything to do with you."

Lisa nodded.

"What are you going to do?" Her mother sounded suddenly alarmed. "Marry him? Paul will never accept your children." She put her hand on Jackie's shoulder. "Whither thou goest, I will go. Your people will be my people. Are you ready for that?"

Paul was standing in the doorway, his arm around Lisa. He blurted out, "For Christ's sake, don't marry him."

"Like I believe in the institution of marriage." Jackie wanted to laugh. Marry him? What made them think *he* would marry *her*? She just needed a place, a place to stay, a place in the world where she liked herself.

She picked up the first box and took it out to the car, threw it in the trunk. When she turned back toward the house, her mother and Paul were standing in the open double doors. Evening, because of the storm, had come on early. The pyracantha was already in bloom and their dusty smell was made more fragrant by the coming rain.

For some reason, Jackie could suddenly see herself from her mother's point of view. All those years of raising her daughter to become someone else, a woman who would graduate cum laude from law school, or at least marry well, and there she was instead, an angry girl in baggy blue jeans and an old black sweater, a skinny girl who made jewelry in a bead shop and took Spanish and design classes at the junior college. A girl who saw nothing scary about the Mexican side of town.

Jackie wondered if her mother ever wished time could loop back so she could say, why are you so sad? What can we do about this? But she never had. Instead, she had looked at her daughter and thought, what is wrong with you? Why are you so different? What do you want from me?

Jackie walked past them to get the last box. She could feel her mother grieving, but that wasn't going to change anything. Even if her mother finally said what was in her heart, it wouldn't change a thing. It was too late. Too little, too late, Jackie wanted to say to her, meanly. Too little, too late. But she said it only to herself, to steel herself for the long drive down to Armando's apartment where, if she were lucky, he would let her in.

in box canyon

There was the time Tomás locked her out of the bathroom. They had been kicking, three days clean, when he walked in with a shit-eating grin. Meant only one thing. Lori's stomach knotted with anticipation. She tried to picture the counselor at the detox center, Jimmy, what he had said, but she could see only the way he had pressed his hands together, fingertip to fingertip, pulsing, a black butterfly.

Maybe he'd said: Straight life is achingly boring. How often can you go to the zoo?

Maybe: Tomás, you need to work.

True, Lori had thought, watching Jimmy press the tips of his forefingers against his lips as he mused on their future, Tomás had always worked. Even when he first got back from Nam. Even when he was sick. Sometimes, if she managed to hustle up some money, she'd take him a paper and a sandwich out to the construction site. It was easy to spot him: he was the tall skinny Mexican with the long ponytail. The good-looking one. It was like a picnic. They'd find a back room, a walk-in closet maybe, away from everyone. They'd squat in the sawdust, hover over the spoon, draw the warm liquid up, get off, and then, while they were eating their chips and drinking soda, they'd kiss.

His dark eyes. Illicit.

Maybe: Lori, you have to stop self-medicating.

Whatever that meant.

There had been a reason they decided to quit, she knew, but it seemed tiny as an ant. *There's going to be only one thing you want to do.* For sure, he'd said that.

She went into the kitchen and lit her cigarette off the flame of the stove. Filled her lungs with smoke. She exhaled, still deciding. What was wrong with a little chemical Nirvana? You just had to keep it under control. Which was why you went through detox, anyways.

Tomás shut the bathroom door softly behind him.

It was locked. She tapped with her fingernails. Their favorite code. He didn't answer. She knocked. Nothing. She banged on the door with the palm of her hand.

"Go away, Lori."

She leaned her forehead against the wood of the door. She couldn't believe it.

"I won't do much," she pleaded.

The smell of sulfur. Her stomach knotted.

"Just save me a taste. Just save me a taste in the cotton."

But he wouldn't open the door. He didn't say another thing. He didn't save her even the smallest taste.

That was the first time she ever hit him. He walked out of the bathroom rubbing his face and she hit him.

"I thought you wanted to stay clean," he said and she slugged him as hard as she could on the arm.

"Don't do me any favors," she told him.

He sat on the sofa and turned on the TV. He picked up a glass of flat soda and took a drink of it. He wouldn't look at her.

She went down to the pay phone. It was next to the lobby, you could see the old pool, how it had been filled in with dirt. The chrome handles of the ladders looked as if they led down into some underworld. Maybe if there were water, cool splashes of blue, shrieks of children, her life could be different. But there was no water. It was summer. Wrong time of year to kick, if you asked her. The sun, the light, all unrelenting. Like a vampire, she longed for her dark cocoon. The pay phone was too hot to touch.

"Listen, Bob, I've been thinking about you a lot, lately and I'd like to get together… but right now I'm kind of sick. You think you could help me out?"

He said, "I told you, babe, smack's a bad scene." That was how he talked. Like an acid head, a hippy, and here it was 1973. He probably still wore that jacket with the peace sign, the Nehru shirts. His red wavy hair down to his shoulders. He'd always reminded her of a buffalo.

They met at a bar, O'Leary's, peanut shells on the floor. He had a moustache. It was kind of comforting to see him, high school all over again, just seeing him. They sat in a booth and he told her about a radio play he was writing.

She leaned her head against the wall and listened. He sure could talk, he sure could make one beer last a long time. Talk about nursing it. She started wondering why she didn't write any more. "Hmmm," she said, "radio play." Who ever heard of such a thing? But she wanted Bob to think she was entertaining his ideas. She wanted him to think he was doing her a favor.

"Aren't you going to buy me another drink?" She touched his hand with her finger, looked straight in his eyes and smiled.

"Sure," and then this look of concern came over his face. "How bad off are you?" He turned his hand over and clasped hers.

"Oh, not so. I'm trying to kick. I just need to do a little, you know, take the edge off." She took her hand back and lit a cigarette. "I'm cutting down gradually."

She held out the pack to him but he shook his head, no.

"You still living with that Mexican dude?"

She shrugged. Mexican dude. He made it sound like an outlaw life. Maybe it had been. Before detox. She missed going down to Mexico. Among other things.

"Don't you think you should get some help?"

"I'm on the waiting list."

He sighed, pulled out his wallet. Twenty bucks. "Promise you'll pay me back," he said, his hand on the bill in the middle of the table. "Not cuz I need it, but because you need to pay it back. That's just part of getting clean. Part of getting in the real world."

She slid the twenty out from under his fingers. "How come you know so much about it?"

He looked a little surprised. "I didn't mean it that way."

"Right." She downed the rest of her drink and then gave him a tight smile.

"Well, you know I'm good for it."

He walked her out to her car, his arm around her shoulders. "I'll see you in a coupla days?"

"That's the deal."

"Promise?" He pulled her toward him. "What's happened to you? How'd you get this way?"

"Nothing so bad has happened."

He stroked her cheek with the back of his hand. She could tell he wanted to kiss her.

She ducked away. God, what did he think? If he screwed her, she would suddenly see the light? She wouldn't want dope any more? Shit.

When she got back, Tomás was still watching television. She got the works and went into the bathroom. Tied off with a belt, held the end of it with her teeth. She stuck the needle in, not far enough, it wouldn't register. She broke out in a sweat, her hand was shaking. Damn. It was so much easier to let Tomás do it. She stuck it in again, but when she tried to register, it slipped out of the vein. Then again, too far, it went through the vein, and a bruise immediately welled in a small lump around the needle. Finally, she got it right. It registered, she loosened the belt a little and pushed the plunger in. God. Lightning traveled up her spine and blossomed. Light filled her head. It was heaven. She didn't need anybody. She didn't need Tomás at all.

In the living room, Tomás said, "How much did you do?"

She opened her eyes. "Enough."

The world had lost its horizontal hold and so she closed her eyes again. She was dreaming about red houses, white shutters, velvet lawns and orange poppies, vermilion poppies, opening again and again. Palm trees against a Technicolor sky. The sound of water rushing, there were cliffs, huge black boulders jutting out of turquoise water, the water swirling and frothy.

"You messed up your arm."

He picked her arm up under the elbow and ran his finger over the vein.

She brought her arm back to her, it hurt. The gray beach was Trinidad, not San Diego; the sandpipers running in and out with the waves, that was San Diego. Trinidad was black rocks, white driftwood, she and her mother had walked down the path through the rain forest, redwood, nettles, blackberries, their fingers stained, their mouths, those black spiders won't hurt you, no poisonous spiders here, her mother had said, the smell of redwood and decay.

"You messed up your arm." His hand was shaking her shoulder. "How much did you do?"

"I did a lot. So much I'm going to die."

"Come on, quit fooling around. Are you okay?"

She pulled him down close to her. She wanted to bite him. "Don't ever screw me over like that again. I hate it."

"I know."

She pulled him closer, until his face was next to hers.

"I want to go away," she told him, "to the ocean."

She loved the winter storms, how they came all the way up to the top of the cliffs in Northern California and left that wood, burned white with salt, how they sounded like thunder, those storms. She closed her eyes and dreamed about California. About an earthquake. This shaking, everything, all the books and dishes shaking on the shelves and she was trying to hold it all together. She could see her hands, trying to hold everything together. But it kept falling apart. And then her hands became Jimmy's hands, pressed together like a butterfly, and she knew it was true, they had to get out of town.

They decided to go camping instead. Tomás wanted to go up into the hills, up this road he knew, away from the other campers, then down a smaller river, down a stream, really, past these old houses that had crumbled down, to these Indian writings on cliffs. He said it would be better there. There was this box canyon, they could walk down it for miles. I've never found the end, he said. They left the dirt road after a while and drove down a dry wash, sandy for a few miles, then through a thicket of mesquite. Tomás ducked as the branches whipped into the cab of the truck. Through the mesquite, up on the banks of the wash, Lori could see grass so green it hurt her eyes. Cows grazing. The walls of the old ranch houses, crumbling adobe, and a windmill.

As they climbed in elevation, they came to a rocky part of the wash and found themselves in a small canyon, the walls burnt red sandstone and banded here and there with black rock. The ocotillo were like skinny fingers reaching for the light, their blossoms bright orange in the dusk. The water was running slightly, just enough to make the tires slick on the rocks, and sometimes they slid, barely missing the boulders that jutted up as the canyon narrowed.

A little farther down, one wall of the canyon disappeared as a smaller branch of the wash emptied into this one. There, in that fork, there was a grassy bank and huge mesquite trees. Tomás drove the truck up the side of the wash and parked beneath the largest tree. They got the food out of the truck, cracked open a few beers and went out to look for firewood because soon it would be too dark to find any. They made a huge fire and cooked a steak and a can of beans. The bats swooped down through camp and Lori put a bandanna over her head so their feet wouldn't get caught in her hair. They watched the fire for a while, the sparks flying up, and took some shots of tequila to take the edge off.

When they walked out away from the fire to look at the stars, she asked him to put his arm around her and they stood there, looking up. There were so many stars, as many as when she was a child, the night sky, whirling and endless. She used to spend hours lying outside at night, beneath a sky filled with stars. It had terrified her, really, because the stars might be dead, their light burned out a long time ago and now barely reaching earth. Even then, even when she was little, she wondered about darkness.

They decided to take their sleeping bag and a blanket down to the wash to make their bed. They smoothed out the sand and spread the sleeping bag out for the bottom. She put her head on his shoulder. It was so quiet. She closed her eyes and listened. The wind sounded like water, and they could hear the bats, a coyote, now and then cattle. The world seemed so calm in the cool night air, but it wasn't calm. Every day someone else came back from the war. Like Tomás, they had their stories, they had their scars, they had china white. They came back to nothing, to a city that was ringed with missiles. Planes, like dark predators, circled overhead. Lori imagined them falling from the sky.

Tomás stroked her hair away from her forehead, something her father used to do when she was little, when he came in to say goodnight and she was falling asleep. It had always made her feel safe, cherished.

Tomás, his face in shadow, the night sky over his head. He kissed her and his lips were cool. When they made love, under the stars, something she had always wanted to do, she found she was crying. She didn't know why. There was just this big gap in her heart, like she'd been hurt, or as if she were afraid. The way she'd felt when her parents kicked her out, maybe. But that was betrayal. Emptiness. She turned her face away from him, the tears leaking from her eyes and running over the bridge of her nose. She didn't want him to know she was crying, but she was afraid he was going to die soon and then there would be no one who loved her. She was afraid he would die, young, because he was good. That was one thing her mother had always said: the good die young.

He asked her what was wrong but she just shrugged. He lifted her up so that her head was resting on his shoulder, but she turned a little, with her back to his side and wrapped his arm around her. She kissed the smooth inside of his arm and looked out at the night. The cottonwoods were rustling all around them. They were far away from everything. If someone dropped a bomb on Tucson, they wouldn't even know. They could go on living there, like people had a hundred years ago, making flour from mesquite beans, eating the new shoots of the prickly pear and the wild spinach that Tomás had pointed out earlier. They could rebuild using those old walls, find tools that had been discarded years ago, get the old well going.

The dark trees on the other side of the wash looked mysterious, as if they held the key to something in their thick and tangled limbs. The sand was dappled with shadows from the dim light of the moon, a waning moon. She listened to his breathing. He had already fallen asleep. Soon he would begin twitching. Then the nightmares. But what was her excuse? It would be so much easier to forgive herself if she could take her finger and point to one day on a calendar: here, she would say, here is when it happened. Or to a part of her body, like the smooth shrapnel scars on Tomás' back: here it is, the source of my pain. My nightmare. But instead, it was only fear, she guessed. That whatever she had would be taken away from her. That the darkness of the world would close in and crush her heart.

In the morning, they hiked up the canyon to see the Indian drawings. When they started out, the canyon was still in shadow and so, a little later, they got to see the sun rise again, over the east wall. They sat on a huge boulder and ate some oranges. They watched the water sliding over the rocks for a few minutes and then Tomás held out his hand and they walked farther up the canyon toward the pools where the drawings were. He told her that he thought the Indians must have camped there in the summers. "There's water nearly year-around and, if you climb up there," he pointed up the steep wall of the canyon, "you'll be on a plateau where you can see for miles."

It was almost noon by the time they got to the pools. The petroglyphs were on the other side of the pools from them, on walls of light-colored sandstone. They were black, geometric drawings, not primitive animal or human shapes like she had expected. On the side of the canyon where they were standing, he showed her scooped-out holes in the rocks, like bowls, *metates*, where the Indians had ground their corn and mesquite beans.

She took off her shoes and dragged her toes along the top of the pool. Splashed some water at him.

"This one's deep enough for swimming," he said.

She looked around. The wall of the canyon where the petroglyphs were was steep, almost a sheer drop and the wall behind them, which had a more gradual incline, was covered with vegetation. It was pretty secluded. He had already undressed and was walking into the water. He hooted and then splashed her. She looked around again and then quickly took her clothes off, did a shallow dive to get it over with. Cold, cold. It took her breath away. He was laughing at her while she gasped for air.

She did another dive, down through the water with smooth motions, trying to disturb the water as little as possible, because she wanted the pool to stay clear and calm so she could see the stones on the bottom. When she surfaced, he was standing, looking at the drawings. She let the reflection—the side of the canyon, the mesquite, the cactus, the sky—come back together, then she dropped the stone she'd brought up and watched the surface break with ripples, watched it become complete again.

She swam over to him and pressed up against him to get warm, rested her arms on his shoulders. Leaned back to look at the drawings. He started to say something but then they both heard a horse snort, hoofs stumble on rock and, when they looked up at the wall behind them, there were three Mexican cowboys on horseback on a trail near the rim of the canyon.

"How long have they been there?" she asked him, but he was studying them. They had rifles on the sides of their saddles.

"They're probably from a ranch around here. *Mojados*."

The cowboys kept looking down at the two of them, their expressions more curious than threatening as if they'd come across a strange animal that didn't belong in the landscape. One of them laughed. They reined their horses and turned to go on toward the end of the canyon. Tomás walked out of the pool and pulled his pants on. Threw Lori her shirt. "They might be back by pretty soon," he said.

They ate the *burritos* they'd brought and then lay back on a boulder. The sun felt good, her cheeks were burning, she put her arm over her eyes and listened to the wind and water, the birds, a fly buzzing. He was so quiet, she thought maybe he'd fallen asleep, but then he said, "I've been seeing this more and more lately, we're not good for each other. Out here, it's easy. But at home, we just bring each other down."

By the sound of his voice, she knew he meant this. She waited for her heart to stop, for him to say more, but he didn't.

She rolled on her side so she could see him. She had to wait for her eyes to get used to the sunlight; she had to be able to see his face, his eyes, so she could know exactly how to register this information. "You want to break up?"

"Until we're both clean."

"I don't believe it. You just made up your mind for both of us?"

He put his hand on the back of her neck, but she shrugged it off.

"This is because of Bob, isn't it?"

"No, that isn't it." He began tossing pebbles at the other side. You're going to start an avalanche, she wanted to yell at him, like her mother used to tell her when she was little and threw stones off the edge of a cliff, but she didn't. She started to cry instead, that noiseless crying where the tears slide out of their own volition and your throat gets so tight you don't think you'll be able to say a thing. She couldn't believe he would do this to her.

"You did it first," she said, her voice, all choked. She hated herself for it. For the way she immediately crumbled.

He threw another stone.

She started wiping the tears off her cheeks with her hands. "You don't love me any more."

He threw a larger stone. It hit right above a drawing, bounced off a boulder and then plunked into the pool. "It's just as hard for me," he said.

"*It's just as hard for me*," she mimicked him and immediately hated the sound of her own voice. It echoed, if not in the canyon, then in her own mind, snotty, like a little kid's. "God," she hit his arm, "it's so like you. You fucking do this to me. *We have to break up*. You don't even ask me what I think about it."

He stood up and started pacing back and forth across a small sandy space. He wasn't about to argue, he was like that.

"You did it first. You're leaving me like I was the one. Like I started you off again. It wasn't my fault."

"Why do you think I want to do this? Look at you. You're too good for this shit, look at you." He took a strand of her hair and rubbed it between his fingers. "You're too tender, or something. This shit's killing you."

He was quiet, like he thought he'd made his best point. Argument over.

She swished her hands around in the water and then held them, cold and wet, against her face. She could hear the *mojados* go by on their horses again, their voices, the hoofs clanging on rock. Her head was pounding. She knew he would do it. He would leave her if he thought it would *save* her. How stupid was that?

"Please," she said, "Tomás. *Please.*"

just family

Rachel was the one who delivered the message. In the middle of dinner, she remembered the phone call, stood up, tossed her braid over her shoulder, and dug in her pocket for a scrap of paper. "Mom," then she looked at her father, "Dad, the prison called again today." She squinted at her eight-year-old scrawl. "They said Uncle Tony gets out tomorrow afternoon. He can be picked up at the a-n-n-e-x."

Ellen sighed. "You remember your Uncle Tony," she said, keeping her voice light, wanting to reassure her daughter. She knew she should be feeling, if not elated, then at least relieved, as if the long ordeal were finally over and Tony could rejoin the living. After all, in the cosmic scheme of things, his crimes were like the buzzing of a gnat. She knew this. Still. She knew what prison could do to a man, remembered all the guys they'd known in the old days, how they came out jumpy as hell. Mean. Just like when guys got home from Nam. No telling what would set them off. And, like them, Tony was being released to nothing: no home, no wife, no friends, a daughter he didn't even know. Nothing. *Nada*.

But Rachel just shrugged. What was there to remember? She was only three when he got sent up. Five years ago. They'd only been to visit him once.

117

"It'll be okay, *mi'ja*," Richard said. "You'll see." Then, to Ellen, "My mom has already asked if he can work with me." He raised his eyebrows. What could he do? Tony was his little brother. He got up and opened the refrigerator. Popped open a beer. Surveyed his garden out the back window. The corn was just coming up. His nana had always had a garden when he was a child, tomatoes climbing rickety stakes. *Yerba buena* beneath the faucet. Chard and *chiles* and hollyhocks. He and Tony had often hidden between the rows. He couldn't remember a time before Tony was born.

Daniel looked up from his spaghetti. "What?" he asked, his mouth full, sauce smeared on the corners of his lips.

"Your Uncle Tony is getting out."

"Oh, oh," he said, "better hide the checks." He was kidding; he liked Tony. At eleven, he remembered his uncle, how he took him to see *Star Wars*, over and over, no matter how many times Daniel asked.

"What if we don't *want* him to get out?" Rachel's shoulders were still hunched in a shrug.

Richard sighed. "Guess I'd better fix the lock on that door."

"Put bars on the windows," Daniel laughed.

"Warn the neighbors." Ellen went along. But what would she tell them if there were suddenly a series of break-ins? Oh, don't worry. It's just my brother-in-law. He only takes what he can carry. He doesn't have a car.

Richard killed his beer. "It'll be all right," he said again. He threw the can in the trash and then walked out the front door, stood in the yard. The neighbor kids were riding their bikes on the sidewalk, zooming in and out of the street to pass one another. To Richard, suddenly the place seemed foreign. Not like the barrio he'd grown up in where everyone had known everyone for generations. Here, people moved in for a few years. Until their kids were grown. He guessed it was like any working-class neighborhood in America: narrow streets lined with trees, small houses constructed of red brick or burnt adobe or siding. In the evenings, men parked their work trucks along the sidewalk; women still hung clothes on the line; children whooped and hollered until dusk. The last few years, though, you could see things going downhill. Broken windows got boarded up instead of replaced. People were keeping their trucks until the wheels fell off. Hell, it was hard for him to find enough work—for an ex-con, like Tony, it would be impossible, and, Richard figured, with a guy like Reagan in office, things would get worse before they got better. He didn't have any choice but to help Tony out.

Otherwise. *Quien sabe?*

When Richard walked back into the kitchen, he put his hands on Ellen's shoulders and then kissed the top of her head before sitting back down at the table. She traced the knobby bone on his wrist. His fingers were absently tapping the smooth wood of the table. A few petals from the bouquet of bougainvillea next to him drifted down to the table and scattered, the thin petals veined like leaves, curling brown on the edges. She'd bunched them into a vase, the clusters spilling over, magenta against the white wall. Behind him, the glass doors and fawn haze of twilight. His dark hair, Daniel's, Rachel's, the reddish tints the light made. All of it could be so easily disturbed, a stone tossed into a pool, but she knew they couldn't lock Tony out of their lives any more than they could stop the flooding back of memory. And that was the intrusion she feared, the intrusion of the past. She and Richard had done many of the same things Tony had done, only they quit and he got caught—and now he'd spent five of the past eight years in prison.

She had this weird feeling—it wasn't déja vù, exactly, it was more like she could suddenly see her life as a time traveler might see it. She could see Richard as he was, a man in his early thirties, lines at the corners of his eyes. His hair was short. And there she was, no longer rail thin. She was someone's mother. Two someones. How did we get here, she wondered, in this house, parents of two children?

It was almost as if time had no continuum; it wasn't a line but a dimension and it had cracked and let Richard and Ellen walk into the room—Richard and Ellen when they were *young*. Long hair, confusion in their eyes. Those ghosts of themselves wandered around the house, from room to room, dazed. Shit, they said, can you believe it?

The next day Ellen called in sick and kept the kids out of school. They packed some fruit, nuts, and water in a daypack and drove up to the state park. It was a perfect day, a clear sky, cool air even though the sun was already warm. They walked slowly up the paved road that took them into the canyon. Every now and then they stopped and looked at the saguaros. Soon, Ellen told them, the flowers would bloom, crown them. She pointed out the new buds on the thin branches of the ocotillo. The grass was a tender green, the poppies and yellow paper flowers in bloom.

After a while, they decided to climb up a large ravine. They had to hop on the rocks to cross the stream. Daniel climbed well, but Rachel needed a little help up the huge granite slabs. "Lean into the mountain," he told her. A few times, he stood on the top of the boulder and held his hand out to Ellen. He picked out a trail, holding back branches of acacia and creosote as Ellen and Rachel followed.

After about fifteen minutes, they rested on a large slab of rock. Daniel said he thought they were the only ones who had ever climbed that far. Rachel started collecting small pieces of quartz that were imbedded with mica. She wanted to know if she'd found silver. Ellen wondered when children got used to the world. When did they stop seeing? She told them she wanted them to notice everything around them. "Even the way the light is," she said. She said she wanted them to think about important things. "Not just who you like or who likes you. Or what clothes to wear." She told them to look at the mesquite trees, how they were a velvety color of green you saw only in early spring.

Rachel stuffed her rocks into a pocket of the daypack. "But I *do* wonder who likes me," she said.

Daniel threw a small stone. It arced out and just missed the stream below. "What Mom means is she wants us to think about the world and the ecosystem and things like that."

"I know." Rachel gave him a dark look. "One time I even asked her who made it so a tree is called a tree and a cat a cat and not the other way around."

Ellen wanted to laugh—Rachel was competitive about everything—but, instead, she put her hand on her arm. "Shh. A cardinal." They watched the bright red as it flashed through the green of the canyon and then Daniel went back to throwing stones and Rachel to collecting them.

"I don't like Uncle Tony," Rachel said suddenly, plopping down next to Ellen. "I don't like people who hurt my nana."

"Maybe you don't remember any good things about him," Ellen said.

"Like what?"

"Oh, like he likes ketchup on his bologna sandwiches. Instead of mayonnaise."

"That's a *good* thing?"

"He can do card tricks," Daniel said.

"He likes those shows about animals on TV," Ellen said.

Rachel scrunched up her face.

"Once he took Steph and me to the zoo," Daniel said.

"He has a sickness," Ellen said. "He never should have gone to jail."

120

"Oh." Rachel was quiet for a while. "It's because he's Mexican, huh? That's why they sent him."

Ellen laughed. "Now, you sound like your father." She pulled out some oranges and began to peel them. It was so quiet she felt as if they were alone in the canyon, as if time were suspended, and she wanted to hold on to that moment of peace, of simply being with them. To memorize it. She knew they would grow too fast. Away from her. She would have to let them go out into the world. She wouldn't be able to keep them safe. Not even from themselves. Not even from their own dangerous inclinations.

They were already, each of them, so separate from her, different from both her and Richard. And it bothered Richard, a little, she knew, that they were not like him, not Mexican enough—really, she supposed, that was the way to put it. That was what bothered him. Especially about Daniel. Daniel with his hair cut skater-style, and his long colorful shorts and big tee shirts. He looked like a kid from one of those big houses in the foothills. Ellen could see him through Richard's eyes, almost as someone else's child, a child who had never been deprived of anything—who had never been hungry or without suitable clothing, who had never been discriminated against. He had never known any of the pain that still colored Richard's childhood, and while that was exactly what Richard wanted, what he had worked so hard to provide, she knew it also worried him. He was afraid Daniel would grow up weak, that he would become just the kind of man Richard scorned. You should see them, he'd say of the college kids who worked for him in the summers, they've had everything handed to them. They don't know what it means to work. And you should hear them put us down. They're not going to be in construction all their lives.

Look, she'd tell him, the kids I work with at the store are the same way. Give them time. At eighteen I'd always had everything I needed. Suffering doesn't necessarily make you a good person.

But she knew he imagined her childhood as always smooth, like the water of the pool in her parents' back yard. She had her own bedroom, a car at sixteen. A gasoline credit card. You were spoiled, he always told her.

When he and Tony were young, their family lived in the back of an old Chinese grocery. The grocery had been boarded up years before when one of the grocers was murdered with a cleaver. Richard said that at night the lights in the grocery would suddenly go on, even though there was no longer any electricity in that half of the building. On some nights, they could hear the cleaver clacking on wood. Another time they lived in an old house with wooden floors and a fireplace. The fireplace turned out to be fortunate because, more often than not, the electricity, water and gas were turned off. Their mother cooked in the fireplace. He remembered her leaning over and lifting the lid to check on the beans. He remembered walking next door with a bucket to get water from their neighbors' faucet. At dusk, he used to run down the alley to the store for milk and the *winitos* who hid in the bushes reached out and grabbed at him. In the morning, a *winito* or two, maybe the same ones, knocked at their back door and his mother gave them cups of coffee and pieces of tortilla or bread. When his father came home late at night from the cantinas, he told them stories about *la llorona*, the coyote, the girl who danced with the devil. Richard remembered only parts of those stories, but they all remembered the hole in the wooden floor and the cat that came up one night and sat on their father's chest as he slept, trying to suck the breath out of him. They all remembered being hungry.

Ellen sometimes wondered if she had married Richard because his childhood was more interesting than hers. Exotic. Not only that, but it had a certain clarity hers lacked. His memories were definite and hard-edged, they had the quality of stories, while hers were impressionistic, dark colors. In his, there was good and evil, personified: cats who might be the devil. In hers, everything was blurry, shapes suggested by color or shadow, and underneath, always, her father's drinking, her mother's bitterness. An angry silence. There was no story. Everything remained unspoken. When they finally broke up and sent her to boarding school, she'd been relieved, not lonely. Even her mother's threat of disinheritance, when she eloped with Richard, was no obstacle. Ellen had seen it as final rupture, a declaration of independence neither she nor her mother could ever go back on. Richard's family was her family now, her chosen family, his brother and sisters substitutes for those she never had.

Not only had he grown up in a different world than she had but, in some ways, she thought, he still lived in a different world. He always said he knew, by feelings, what would happen and what would not. He knew when his grandmother was going to die because he dreamed that some neighbor women came and stood outside her fence. They were dressed in black and they were throwing stones at the house and a week later his nana died from an operation. The night Tony's best friend died, Richard dreamed the death, the details of the overdose, the bathroom, the police, all clear in his mind. Before Tony got sent up, Richard dreamed about a painting by Diego Rivera, the one with a white wall, a window that looks out on nothing, a black revolver on the windowsill.

She often thought of these things, past dreams and past events, and told herself they proved nothing, they didn't determine the present or the future. But sometimes, at night, lying in the darkness next to Richard, she'd know they were right. She knew because before she fell in love with him, she had a dream that he came to her and said, everything will be all right. In the dream, they were flying through darkness, they were lying down, flying among the stars, and he put the palm of his hand against her cheek. He whispered it again: "Everything will be all right."

A few weeks later, when Richard brought Tony by the house, Ellen couldn't help but be surprised by his pale skin, by how much weight he'd gained. Richard was much thinner than Tony now, and much darker, from working out in the sun. Tony's hair was curlier, it had always been curlier, wild sometimes, but now it was short, slicked back.

"Whew," he greeted her with a bear hug. "Looking go-od."

"Gained some weight," she laughed. "But then so have you."

He laughed and a curl fell down on his forehead; he shook it back in place with one movement. Pachuco style. He had a tattoo on his forearm. She remembered him without it. And when he spoke, he spoke with an accent, something he had never done before. In prison, it was important to be part of *la raza*.

Ellen set out chips and salsa, got them each a beer, and then joined them in the living room. They talked for a while, mostly Richard and Tony talked about work, and then Tony said, "Remember that guy Reid?"

Richard nodded absently and picked up the sports section. He didn't want to talk about the old days any more. All day at work, for the past week, it was all Tony had wanted to do, tell him about the guys they'd known who were now in the joint, or tell him about his new *carnales*, his brothers. That was how he talked. Hey, bro. It bothered Richard no end. He hoped it was some kind of re-entry phenomenon.

"Reid's dead," Tony said, "they found him in Nogales. In an alley. They just dumped him there. He'd OD'd and they didn't even try to revive him. Just took his dope and his money and left him in the alley." He looked at Richard for a reaction. "They didn't find him for days."

"And? What did you expect?"

Tony gave a low whistle. "That's cold, man." He shook his head at Ellen. "Can you believe how cold some people are? He was there for days. Until these dogs started dragging him out."

Richard lifted the newspaper in front of his face again.

"The last time I saw Reid was when we visited you guys up at the Fort," Ellen said. "That picnic we had, remember?" They had brought food and spent the day in the visitors' yard, gathered around the long picnic tables at the minimum-security prison. She had been surprised Tony and Reid could be friends there. Especially after the things she'd heard about the prison in Florence. Tony couldn't talk to whites or blacks at Florence, not even if he'd known them on the outside, but when he got transferred to minimum security, the Fort, he'd said it wasn't as bad.

The funny thing was, Ellen had known Reid long before she ever met Richard and Tony. She always remembered him in a car, driving fast, one hand on the wheel, blond hair messy with wind. Then there was the time they were sitting in the park and he rolled up his girlfriend's sleeve to show Ellen where he'd stabbed her with a syringe, over and over, these dime-sized purple bruises. There were some things she preferred *not* to remember.

Tony was staring out the window at the leafy branches of the mulberry. At the work trucks lined up and down the street and the kids on their bicycles. He sighed, "You guys have lived in this house a long time."

He looked *desorientado*, like he was a foreigner or, more likely, as if the passage of time had just registered. She was about to say something. Maybe about the tree, or living there, maybe simply about the past, it's behind us, everything has changed. Time to move on, Tony.

He sighed, "I called over at Jenna's mom's house yesterday and they wouldn't let me talk to her. Hell, even in prison, you get visitors."

He walked around the room. Picked up the picture on the bookcase, the one Ellen had taken of Stephie with Daniel and Rachel for his mother.

"Look, I was understanding. I told her, you do what you've got to do. When I get out, we'll put things back together. But now I'm out, I see how it is." When neither Richard nor Ellen responded, he walked over to the window. "Shit, she could at least let me see Stephie."

Richard was scanning some stats on the sports page; he didn't want to touch this one. Neither did Ellen. They both knew Tony could be explosive on the subject of Jenna. After all, he had taken the fall for her and she had divorced him almost as soon as he got sent up.

Tony lit a cigarette. "It's like this, when I was in there, I knew it was hard for her. I told myself, fucking is only fucking, but she'd better not give her love away."

Richard sighed. "Somehow I always thought the two were connected."

"What world do you live in?" Tony blew smoke out in an angry stream.

Richard put the newspaper down. "So what do you have to learn in this life? Patience?"

Tony jerked his head back. "What's that supposed to mean?"

"You know. All the time you've had to sit and wait. Because of all the times you've made other people miserable."

Tony's laugh was quiet. "Well, maybe that's why I'm here, big brother. I'm your punishment. For all those things you did." He narrowed his eyes at Richard. "*Veras?*"

"Right. That makes all kinds of sense."

Ellen stood up and put her hand on Richard's shoulder. "Oh, I don't know," she said, trying to smooth everything over. "I figure it doesn't matter so much where you end up so long as you do something in life."

"My philosophy exactly. Life is like a train. You may as well enjoy the ride." Tony grinned at her and sat back down. "And that's just what I plan on doing."

The sudden shift of perspective, how he turned everything around, that's what bothered her. She sat on the arm of Richard's chair. "I hope things work out for you," she told him. But she knew he heard something else: don't fuck us over. Ever again.

"Tony could stay clean," Richard said, "if only he had a memory."

He was lying in bed when he said this. Ellen had just slipped in, her skin was cool next to his and she smelled like rosewater—clean, but not sweet. It was the same soap his family had used when he was a child and so he didn't know what made him feel calm—Ellen next to him, or the scent—not that it mattered. What mattered was that he felt calm, cared for, part of someone else's life. As he had as a child. As he did every night when she slid into bed. That's what he meant about Tony. There were things that provided continuity, scents were one of them, memory another, and continuity gave you a home, not only in the world, but in the larger scheme of things.

Ellen rolled over, facing him. His breathing was so quiet, she thought he had fallen asleep, but he was lying on his back, his eyes open in the dim light from the window.

"But he never remembers anything. Or it's all twisted, somehow."

"I know," she said, "the way he was talking about Jenna. He gets out expecting everything to pick up where he left off. All those years, zap, they're gone." For Tony, she thought, there was only the moment. No past, no future. Maybe prison was like dope in that way: you went into another world, time stopped, you came out blinking your eyes.

She ran her fingertips up and down Richard's bare chest. It was sad, all so sad. Tony had taken the rap for Jenna so she could take care of their little girl; then she gave Stephie to her mother and turned her back on him. Like that. His sacrifice meant nothing. Tony, living in that cell for five years, no one to touch him in tenderness. What did that do to a person, she wondered, not only the deprivation of the natural world—sky, sun, wind, plants—but of human touch? A kind word. Someone to confide in.

"What am I afraid of, anyways?" she asked suddenly. "We don't have the kind of things he would steal."

"I don't know about you," Richard whispered, "but I'm afraid he'll start again. And then we'll lose him," he sighed. "I'm afraid he's going to die."

She wished she could be as good as Richard but she could foresee a time where Tony's death might seem inevitable. A relief, even. And, yes, she knew why Richard felt guilty. They had done their share of experimentation, but they'd never *hurt* anyone.

"God," he sighed, "God, I regret those years."

"What does that mean?" she asked him. "That you would go back and change your life if you could? You would *be* somebody else?"

He'd always told her, if my parents had just stayed in the barrio, I'd be a doctor, a lawyer, like all my friends from junior high. But no, they moved us to the east side, to the white schools, to keep us out of trouble, give us opportunities, and what did we do? We started hanging out with guys like Reid. That's what drugs do. When you're an outsider, they give you instant community.

She tried to see herself as someone other than who she was, someone who had made other choices, but she couldn't. She could see herself leaning against a wall at school; she was very thin and very smart. She never had to study. She was wearing black, always black tee shirts and navy bell-bottoms; her hair was long and frizzy. She was lost in an opium dream. The other girls walked by in their villager skirts and button-down blouses and Capezios. They carried their pompoms. They giggled when the boys talked, tilted their heads, gazed up at them. But that had never been Ellen's dream. Ellen had never wanted to be like those girls. No, she had wanted to be different. Daring. A risk taker. In her dream, a blue car sped down a curved mountain highway, the ocean on one side, cliffs on the other, the car gliding around the corners. She touched the steering wheel ever so slightly, her hand on the wheel, her long fingers light on the leather, she could almost think the car around the corners.

And then, there was another image, this one from memory: she and Jenna are backing out of Reid's driveway. They're loaded, Ellen's driving. Jenna has just lit a cigarette and handed it to her. Tony comes out to say goodbye and Jenna and Ellen say, high as anything, don't start, Tony, don't ever start. In the rearview mirror, Ellen sees Richard, tall and thin, hair past his shoulders. He's come over to Reid's house to score. Richard. She knows he's Tony's older brother, but she's never really seen him before. Never seen his eyes, how shy they are. The Garcia brothers are both standing next to her car and that's what she sees, Richard's eyes. Tony, Jenna says, don't do it. And yet only a few days later he's sitting in the back seat of a Chevy and Ellen's kneeling on the front seat, facing him. He's wrapped the belt around his arm and pumped up and Reid sticks the needle in Tony's vein. Pulls the plunger back, the blood surges in dark red, then Reid pushes the plunger forward. Ellen's watching Tony's face, waiting to see his eyes pin; waiting, impatiently, for her own rush.

Tony, the last to try it, the first to get strung out. Within a year, he had black marks snaking down his arms. This is important, she thought, it explains our guilt. Or why our complicity feels like guilt.

She pressed her face to Richard's neck. He was her drug now. When he held her at night, she settled in, felt her body all along his, the edge of her self melting into him. Osmosis. He made her feel calm. She exhaled. She felt it. The exhale. Relief. She must have been holding her breath ever since they'd heard Tony was getting out.

Richard couldn't sleep. He kept replaying the eruptions of Tony's anger. Everything was a struggle. Twice Tony had taken a swing at him. Richard was beginning to wonder if it had been a mistake to give him a job, but there was no point in telling Ellen any of this. Although, he supposed, if he lost the job, he might *have* to tell her.

Shit, he couldn't *afford* to lose this job. And all because of Tony's temper. But it hadn't been Tony's fault. Not really. The woman had yelled at him first.

Actually, she had yelled at this *chaparrito* landscaper, not even five feet high, looked Guatemalan, probably didn't speak much English. Maybe not much Spanish. Looked Indian. Richard remembered that he had walked over to the edge of the roof as soon as he'd heard her voice, afraid immediately that Tony had done something. He'd leaned over the parapet wall to get a clearer view. But it hadn't been Tony. There the woman stood, the homeowner, in her turquoise running suit and gold sandals, towering over the landscaper. She was berating him, pointing first at a trench, then at plants someone had trampled, and then right in his face. The landscaper stood, arms folded across his chest, watching her impassively. His calm expression and lack of response was probably making her blood pressure go up by the second.

The confrontation would have ended soon after. That's what usually happened. The homeowners just liked to blow off steam. Or maybe they thought complaining would get them some extras. They hated to pay for the extras, especially the ones who could afford them. They would yell at you, you'd tell them to take it up with the contractor, then the contractor would yell at you. Thing was, they still had to pay and the more they had to pay, the more they wanted to make you pay. So you had to fucking take it. You had to stand there and let them know, that yes, you understood the hierarchy. They had more money than you did, which meant they had more power, which meant they got to be rude. Being rude was part of their privilege. Of course, Tony knew all that as well as he did, but Tony had always made it a point not to buy into any system.

"Look," Tony had pointed to the landscaper's truck, "he *plants* plants." He was speaking very slowly and patiently as if the woman had an IQ of about ten. "He doesn't *trample* plants. And he *doesn't* dig trenches."

Even before Richard had seen the woman's face flame up, he'd known it was too late. He would never be able to get off the roof quickly enough. He watched the landscaper make a quick exit. It was just the woman and Tony now, the trench—thank God for the trench—between them.

She leaned forward and jabbed her finger at Tony. "Well, then, who did it?"

"Satan." Tony hissed, narrowing his eyes. "Satan did it."

The woman's face went momentarily slack from surprise, but she recovered. "We'll see," she snapped. She stalked back towards her house.

"Satan?" Richard asked when he finally made it down the ladder. "Satan? Tucson Power dug the trench."

"Oh, really, Richard? You sure?"

"Fuck, Tony, you can't go yelling at the homeowners. Even if they are idiots."

"Did I yell?" he yelled. "You call that yelling?"

"Calm down!" Richard had looked over at the woman's house.

"You fucking calm down!" Tony had then stomped off the job.

Richard couldn't believe it. He climbed back up the ladder. He was going to have to try to finish alone. Of course. And, of course, soon after the incident, a truck pulled up in the driveway. It was Earl, the project supervisor, laconic and weary, made weary by a job Richard would have hated even more than his own.

"So," Richard said, when Earl came back out of the woman's house, "You the clean-up crew?"

"She swears you got up in her face and threatened her." Earl raised his hand to stop Richard's objections. "I know. I know you. And I know this woman. But she threatened to call the cops. She wants you off the job. Now. "

"I'll leave when I'm finished."

"That's what I told her." Earl looked at her house. "Tough shit, lady." He lifted his cap and scratched his head. "'Course you know I'll hear about this from Tom."

"Sorry. But there isn't a whole hell of a lot I can do about it now."

As Richard walked Earl over to the truck, he'd told him the story. Earl had laughed, "No wonder." Then he climbed in and rolled the window down. "Piece of advice," he'd said, "don't let your brother near the homeowners. Tattoos scare 'em and they sure don't want to hear about Satan."

Richard couldn't sleep. *Satan*? He got out of bed and walked down to the living room and turned the TV on, no sound. The shadows flickered on the walls. Tony talked about Satan all the time now. He'd become a Jesus junkie. Well, no atheists in foxholes or prisons and all that, but how did he get to be so sanctimonious? *A lie weighs the same as murder.* He actually said things like that. Told Richard he'd done time for him, washed away his sins. Ellen's too. Not to mention Jenna's. And in some weird way, Richard knew, he bought into it. He'd often had this idea that he should have gone instead.

The Welcome Home party was just family. Ellen was playing the good hostess. She put a pitcher of margaritas on the table. "Anything else?" she asked. "Before I sit down?"

Tony tapped a pack of cigarettes and said, "Come on, Artie boy, push those chips to the center of the table. You're not afraid of losing, are you?"

He and Richard were sitting at the table with the older sister Grace and her husband Art. They were playing five-card draw. Art had a poker face, the gift of being invisible, until he cleaned everybody out. He was one of those guys who was really good with horses because of some mystical affinity, maybe. And Grace, willful and strong, her thick black hair and long legs, coltish even in her late twenties, was—like Richard always said—the horse even Arturo would never be able to tame.

Art tipped back. He took his time, pushing one chip at a time, slowly, into the pot.

In the kitchen, the younger sister, Amelia, was making potato salad, slicing black olives into the bowl. She was as small and thin as she had been as a girl, less than one hundred pounds and yet she had given birth to two nine-pound babies. Her husband Victor said they inflated upon delivery. Her three-year-old son was pulling on her shirt. Patience, Manny, she said, and then put an olive on each of his index fingers.

Once, before Tony got sent up, when he ripped off their mother's house, he had stolen Amelia's favorite things, a sterling silver dove her *nina* had given her for her first Holy Communion, a pair of jade earrings, and a wooden box her *nino* had brought home from the Philippines. Still, she forgave him without question, as everyone always did, came to the party and made potato salad, and when Tony asked her what she was going to be when she grew up, she just laughed and said, I *am* grown up.

Ellen had told him, with every person you hurt, you hurt yourself. They are what hold you in this world. But he always managed to turn it around: they had never let him into their world, he said.

Tony was saying that he didn't like Salvadorans. "There was this one in jail, cut off a guy's hand with a machete."

"Why'd he do that?" Daniel asked, sitting down.

"When they threw him in the holding tank with us," Tony said, lighting a cigarette, "he was all messed up. They'd beat him up bad. Not the pigs. These guys at a bar. They took him in the john, beat the shit out of him and ripped him off. It wasn't the first time either."

"Sounds like a bright guy," Ellen said, looking at Daniel's face. She wondered if she should let him listen to all of this. "Keeps going back for more."

Tony blew out a stream of smoke and said, "You wanna hear

what happened?"

Grace made a disgusted sound. "Not really."

She was studying Tony. Now that he and Jenna were seeing each other, she was sure he was going to start using again. They all knew the signs. His eyes changed color, to green, and got all pinned when he was loaded. His voice got husky. And then, there would be the more obvious signs, marks on his arms, money borrowed and never paid back. Eventually, missing items. It was sad, but whenever anything was missing, the assumption was as quick and accurate as a heartbeat: Tony.

"So this Salvadoran decides he's not gonna let them push him around. This dude was maybe five two, a little sucker, and he goes home and gets his machete. When he comes back, these dudes are still in the bar, drinking up his money, and he goes up to one of them and pulls the machete out. Well, the guy stands up and tries to shield his head, like so," Tony held his arm in front of his face, "and the machete slices the guy's hand in two, like that, man. Clean. All the fingers gone, the thumb cut in half."

Ellen tried not to see the stump or the blood but her mind worked that way; she could see everything. Not only that, but it brought to mind all the things Tony had told them. How, at Florence, he saw this guy throw kerosene or something in another con's cell, then a match, and the guy's a fireball, locked in, everyone else shouting and banging on the bars, afraid the fire will spread. And another time, how Tony had to shank this guy, a friend on the outside, to prove his loyalty to *la familia*.

Tony, they had said, what happened in there doesn't matter, it's a different world.

But, of course, it did matter. Now that he had been out for a while, it was obvious. What had happened and, especially, what he had done to survive it, weighed him down, kept him there, away from the rest of the family.

"You wanna play, you're gonna pay. That it, Tony?" Richard tapped his cards on the table.

"Anyways, they throw this guy in the tank with us and he wants to plead self-defense. I tell him, you better cop a plea, man, otherwise, they're gonna bury you."

"So?" Richard asked. "Did he cop a plea?"

"Yeah. He got five years." Tony laughed and ground out his cigarette. "One year for each finger."

Art shook his head. "Sounds heavy," he said. He stretched, cracked his knuckles. "Time for some serious poker."

Tony smiled his slow smile. "Get ready to lose."

"Oooh," Daniel said, "I'm scared."

"So," Tony asked Daniel, "you always wear nail polish?"

Daniel shook his bangs out of his eyes and gave Tony a coy look. He had let Rachel practice on him that afternoon. Dark red on his right hand, blue on the left. Ellen remembered them sitting in a square of light on the living room floor. Daniel was watching cartoons. She thought Rachel had even done his toes.

"What's the matter?" Daniel laughed. "Don't you like the color?"

In one swift movement, Tony was standing. He had whipped Daniel out of his chair and was holding him upside down by legs.

"You know what they call people like that?"

"The purple is my favorite," he lisped, still laughing.

"Fags."

"Okay, Tony," Richard said.

But Daniel was not scared. "You should see my toes," he howled.

"Enough," Ellen said, frowning at him in warning. Why did he have to be such a clown?

"Give it a rest," Grace said. "The kid's gonna be an actor."

"You know what happens to them in prison?" Tony shook his head as if he were thoroughly disgusted. He deposited Daniel back in his chair and sat down in his own. "All I'm saying's he should know how the world is."

"At *eleven*?" Ellen asked.

Tony shrugged: *Oh, well. I tried.* He picked up Grace's toddler, Annie, and let her hold his cards. Told her which ones to discard and she slapped them on the table.

Dealer's choice. Daniel called five-card draw, one-eyed jacks wild, and jokers wild in straights and flushes.

Tony leaned back in his chair. "Where are Victor and Amelia? Don't tell me they're keeping their *mota* to themselves."

Grace said, "Amelia is in the kitchen. Pass me the ashtray."

Tony persisted. "Victor and Berto and that guy they brought with them, they're out back toking up, right? Why not spread the wealth around?"

They all looked out the sliding glass door at Victor, Amelia's husband, and his brothers Berto and Chito. They were all huddled in a circle around the brick barbeque, drinking beer. They were dressed in Levis, jean jackets, flannel shirts, and wore their hair long and shaggy, or in ponytails with baseball caps. All except Victor, who had style, who wore his hair short on top and long in back. *Que suave, ese*, Richard and Art teased him. Victor passed a joint and then turned his attention back to flipping the steaks.

Grace said, "If you want to smoke, go outside. Nobody's stopping you."

Art said, "Notice the muscles on that landscaper today? Ever seen a chick with pecs like that?"

Tony's voice got this edge. "You trying to tell me that this kid's never seen anyone smoke pot?"

"*Como chingas.*" Richard put his cards down. "I'm sure he has." He looked at Daniel. "Have you?"

Daniel grinned, "Nah, never."

"Okay, Tony?" Richard's voice was soft. "*Bastante.*"

Tony stood up, bumping the table against Richard, spilling the beer. He tossed his cards in front of Richard and made his voice just as soft. "Fuck you. We're not at work. Don't tell me what to do."

On his way out, he punched the living room wall, and the drywall gave, a small fist-like indentation. The front door slammed. It was quiet except for the sound of the younger children playing in Rachel's bedroom, the fan whirring through the smoky light over the table.

"Temper, temper—huh, Daniel?" Amelia shook her head at him. She was standing in the doorway to the kitchen, wiping her hands on a dishtowel. Richard fished the wet cards out of the beer.

Ellen looked at the dent in the wall. Someday, she thought, we'll have little shelves and pictures in odd places all over our house, just like Richard's mom does, covering all the places where Tony got mad.

Art shook his head, "Hope you guys like knick-knacks."

They all sat back down and Art began the soft shuffling.

Grace looked at Richard, "You and Tony never could get along."

"Sure, Grace, it's my fault."

She waved her hand in the air, forget it. Then said to Daniel, "Did your dad ever tell you how your Uncle Tony used to spend a half hour every morning before school combing his hair?"

Daniel shook his head.

"There were six of us—four kids!—and one bathroom, and he took forever. So when he finally did come out, hair just so, your dad used to," she reached over and tousled Daniel's hair, "do that. And then Tony, crying, would chase him all the way to school."

Richard shook his head. "Remember that game we used to play with the rope, where we held it and the other kids ran and jumped over it? But when it was Tony's turn, we'd yank the rope tight and clothesline him?"

Art and Richard both tipped back in their chairs and laughed. Rachel placed a plate of food on the table in front of Ellen and then climbed up in her lap. "You going to share?" Ellen whispered in her ear. Rachel tore a piece of tortilla, wrapped it around a chunk of barbequed steak, and offered her mom a bite.

"Or the time," Richard said, "when he wouldn't help with the yard work and Grace and I got some of the neighbor kids to help us tie him up. We wanted to hang him upside down from the tree so he'd agree to do the raking."

Daniel looked shocked. "You hung him from a tree?"

Grace laughed. "We tried, well. But he was too heavy."

Richard pointed his beer at Daniel. "He asked for it. That was hard work and he was just sitting there in the shade laughing at us for doing it. One of those palm fronds sliced me a good one, right through my jeans, and that sucker wouldn't help."

Richard sighed, clicked his pop top with his thumb. "Every goddamn thing, no matter how small, Tony's got to tell me I don't know what I'm doing. He knows a better way, a faster way. Finally I told him, look, I've been doing this for years while you've been sitting on your ass in prison."

Art laughed. "Yeah, he sucks you into saying things like that and then he says, fine, fuck you, and walks off the job."

Everyone was quiet, just the shuffling of the cards, a huge moth beating its wings against the glass door. Grace stirred her margarita with her finger, took a sip. "Give him some time."

"Yeah," Amelia said, "he's only been out for a month. He's got to adjust."

Art got up and put his hand on Grace's shoulder. "Time," he said and shook his head, almost as if he were puzzled. "What the hell is more time gonna do?"

"He talks about the joint like it's home. You should hear him, the guys, the guys, the guys." Richard tapped the table for emphasis. "They're his family now."

Grace and Amelia sighed at once.

"He's changed, I'm telling you. Hell, he thinks hot dogs from the 7/11 are *good!*"

Art was the only one who laughed. It was the saddest thing he'd heard yet.

"He got paid today. That's why he was so anxious to leave." Richard folded his cards and looked at Grace. "Don't be thinking everything's gonna be different."

"Well," Amelia said, "I'm hiding my checks." She looked around sheepishly. "I can't afford it, well."

"Listen to us," Grace said, "just listen to us."

They all looked at one another.

"It isn't up to *us*," Ellen said.

There was a longer silence and Richard said. "Yeah, well that's true."

Victor, with Amelia's and his youngest slung over his shoulder, came in from the back. He wore his tee shirt, a black one that proclaimed *Good but not Cheap!* stretched tight over his muscles. "Where'd Tony go?" he asked. "What'd you guys do to him this time?"

They all shook their heads and laughed. Art nodded his head at Richard. "Ask him. It's his fault."

Daniel and Rachel had been absolutely quiet during the whole conversation. Ellen guessed they would learn that there were consequences, certain things you should never try or do or say. Maybe. She hoped that's what they would learn. Maybe they would learn that even adults don't have all the answers. But when Daniel started asking Grace to tell more stories—about the old house, the old neighborhood—Ellen guessed that maybe knowing too much too soon was scary, too. Just as scary as the silence she had struggled to decipher when she was a child.

"Wasn't Beatrice a witch?" he asked Grace.

"That's what they say," she said. "They found a trunk in her house when she died and it was full of books about black magic and full of dolls." She looked around at the kids, "You know the kind they stick pins in? When her son found these things, your tata told him to take them to the priest."

"Once Beatrice gave us these little sacks of herbs, remember, Grace?" Amelia said. "And she hung on them on strings around our necks. We both got really high fevers. I kept dreaming about these women walking around our bed. Women in white gowns. Chanting. Every now and then, they'd reach their hands out at us like they wanted us to come with them." She shivered. "I knew they were dead," she shivered again. "We were so sick and my mom didn't know what to do. But when my dad saw the sacks of herbs, he took them and burned them. Right away, our fevers broke. Remember, Grace?"

"That's not all," Grace said, "when I was going over to Beatrice's, the things I said in anger would come true. For instance, once when Richard refused to give me a ride, I said, I hope you get a flat tire. And he got one. And once, when I was mad at Tony, I went over and put my hand, just my fingertips, really, on the windshield of this car he was sitting in, and the windshield cracked. It wasn't cold outside or nothing. It just cracked." She made this face that said: now you tell me.

Rachel was pressing her back against Ellen's chest as if she'd like to disappear inside her. The other children were gathered around the room, their eyes shining, especially Grace's oldest, Andi, who kept saying, tell us a *story*, Mom, not a *memory*.

"Okay, one," Grace said. The younger children were drifting off to sleep on a quilt she'd spread on the floor in the living room. She looked over at them and then at Andi and Daniel and Rachel, she narrowed her eyes and made her voice low, almost as low as a whisper. "This story is about a girl who wants to go to the dance so badly that she threatens her mother. She says, I don't care what you say, I'm going anyways. And her mother threatens her back. If you go, *mi'jita*, she tells her, I'll lock you out. Don't think I won't. The girl shrugs, she doesn't believe her mother, and she goes to the dance anyways. When she's there, she dances with this very handsome stranger, a man no one has ever seen before, a man no one else will dance with. And they dance all night, twirling around and around, and then, just after the last song, when she turns to say goodbye, he's disappeared. On the way home, she wonders if she'll ever see him again. It's very dark, and it's a long way home and just as she's passing some bushes, she thinks she feels someone walking behind her. She stops, she hears footsteps. Then she turns, and she thinks she sees these red eyes in the darkness, she feels his hot breath. She begins to run faster and faster. Still he's behind her. Faster and faster, she runs. Finally, she reaches her door, but it's locked. She knocks and knocks at the door, she calls for her mother, but her mother wants to teach her a lesson. She won't open the door. She listens and listens to her daughter's cries, to her scratching at the door but, still, she won't let her in. Finally, her daughter is silent. And the mother, thinking she's learned to obey her, opens the door. But her daughter is nowhere to be found. There's no trace of her. No blood, no clothing, no tracks. Nothing. Only the door is torn to shreds. The mother calls out to her. There's no answer. She calls to her neighbors for help and they all call and call for the girl, and search for her, but no one ever sees her again.

"You know," Grace said, looking right into their eyes, one by one, "they say the Santa Cruz used to run all year round. They say there used to be a lake there, in Carrillo Gardens, where the dance was held, but after that night, after the girl danced with the devil, the river dried up. So did the lake. That's what your nana told me, anyways. She told me they never had any dances after that."

Rachel had Ellen's hands pressed firmly over her ears. Ellen cupped her palm and whispered beneath it, "I will never lock you out, *mi'ja*."

As Ellen looked at the sleepy faces of the children, at Grace and Amelia as they lifted their sleeping kids and murmured to them, it's all right, shh, it's all right, she could see what Grace had always seen: there was no way they could give up on Tony. The feeling was, if the fabric of the family held together, they could somehow keep him among the living. But it wasn't just for his sake. Grace wanted the family to stay whole for all of them, for the children. Like her mother, she believed in holding the family together at any cost. One tear and she was afraid it would all begin to unravel.

can you hear me?

Van Garza knew his father was omniscient, that he could see, among other things, the small square adobe house near the university where Van lived with his girlfriend Darlene. He could see the prickly pears, tall as trees, standing guard, and the chili pepper Christmas lights strung around the front window. Sometimes Van listed the things his father would approve of: Van's breakfast, even though it was high fat—after all, fat was *not* what had killed his dad—the time Van painted the house so he could get a month's rent free, the fact that he had taught himself to play guitar, and the frequency with which he made love to Darlene. In death as in life, his father didn't want to know intimate details, which is one reason Van had to jam his signals and banish him from the bedroom, and at times when Van got really lucky from the bathroom and the living room. There were also, of course, things that triggered his father's disapproval: smoking dope. Any kind of dope, actually. No matter how ingested. Tequila. (Which *had* killed him.) The worries Van had heaped upon the shoulders of his mom and twin sister, Zee. And last but certainly not least, the current scheme with James and Jim B.

Van felt his father's presence most acutely when he was making himself breakfast. In the dim natural light of the kitchen, while he let the whites of the eggs sizzle, their round yolks as yellow as the chicks they would not become, while he gingerly heated tortillas on the open gas flame, he felt his father watching. Just over his right shoulder. He slid the eggs out of the pan onto his plate, folded his tortillas in quarters, poured coffee out of the black enamel percolator they'd used for camping, and stirred in the half-and-half. Sometimes he heard his father say his name, Ivan, which in Spanish is *Eevahn*. Softly. *Eevahn*. Sometimes he felt as if he *were* his father, as if he were standing over his own right shoulder watching his hands. Kind of like when he was the sniper: there was the gun, there were the hands, right in front of him, but they weren't his. There was always a moment of disorientation.

He set the plate of eggs on the round, plastic table. The midmorning light was sliding down the window. He rested his forehead against it. Warm already. Next door they were talking about demons again. The woman was wearing a tee shirt that said "SLAVE." The man was lying in the dirt, welding his Harley. Someone, in an announcer's voice, suggested demons were at the heart of the insurgency. In a car up on the next street, a woman was looking for Van. Maybe she was a cop. His eggs were getting cold. He pulled his cell from the pocket of his cargo pants and opened it. No messages from Zee. Izzy. Isabel. She was in Italy. She never answered. Van said her name aloud in Spanish. As their father would have. *Ees-ah-bel*. As if that would call her to him.

§§§

Zee was sitting on a bench high above the small town of Riomaggiore, the southernmost of the five small towns of the Cinque Terre. Below her and beyond (all the way to the coast of Spain, which she could not see), stretched the blue, blue Mediterranean. There was a single red geranium in a pot on the wall in front of her. Behind her, two women, possibly lesbian housewives, she thought, married to men they did not love, were whispering in Italian. They sounded furious, but it may have been passion. Behind them, in the school, small children were singing. Far below, somewhere in the waves, Zee's current (although temporary) Scottish boyfriend was snorkeling beyond the huge black slabs of slate that edged the coast.

She had just snapped closed the fancy cell phone that bounced her mother's voice off a satellite somewhere far above the earth. Van was short-circuiting again. Her mother was frantic. Of course. Van had been off and on anti-depressants, in and out of rehab so often that frantic had become her mother's default mode.

No, Zee told her, she would not cut her trip short.

Sorry, can't hear you, she'd said.

Sorry, you're cutting out.

Which was true. Bad connection. And now the phone said *Emergency Only.* So much for technology. How could air waves be *full*, as in so saturated that not one more voice could come across? Zee didn't get it. But *Emergency Only*, post 9/11, made her slightly nervous and she was not one to be neurotic. Neurosis seemed to her self-indulgent, narcissistic, because like a child, you put yourself at the center of the universe, forces conspiring against you, as if you were more than a speck of sand on a beach of specks. Giving in to unfounded fear was a sign of a weak mind, a failure of logic. This, she firmly believed. Usually she, Isabel, for instance, could flip a switch and turn off her own fears as easily as she could disregard her mother's.

On the other hand, perhaps these fears were *not* unfounded. She had been getting strange text messages. *The world is a lonely planet.* That was the first one. She'd dismissed it as some kind of joke. Van knew she used *Lonely Planet Guidebook*. Stoned, he would think that was clever. It would be his way of saying, 'call me, I'm lonely' without ever having to say 'call me, I'm lonely.'

But, then, this morning, simply: *z can u hear me*

And Zee had to wonder. Maybe he was in some kind of trouble. It would explain the rock in the pit of her gut, the way the hair on her arms had been standing on end. But she still didn't want to go home. Spain was there, she told herself, even though she could not see it. Benjy was swimming, even though she could not see him. Surely, she did not have to see Van standing in the same room to know he was okay. Plus, think about it logically. He was sending text messages from somewhere this side of the great divide between the depressed and the living. When he was really in trouble, they didn't hear from him at all. Have some faith, she wanted to tell her mother, he *is* twenty-three years old.

Cut her trip short? Forget it. This was her idea of heaven: every morning she woke up next to Benjy. He rubbed her back and breathed softly on her neck. He thought she was exotic, *my Mexican-American Barbie doll*, he'd sighed more than once, which was, she knew, insulting in its own way except he meant it as a compliment: because of her long legs. Everything he said, in that Scottish accent, sounded like a compliment. His blue eyes, nearly unblinking behind wire-rimmed glasses, his red hair, spiky and surprised, he always looked at her with a kind of wonder: that she had hooked up with him! Van would never believe that she, a girl who mooned over black basketball players, a girl who found the shaved heads of gang bangers sexy, would end up with lily white, wiry, geek chic Benjamin. But she liked feeling like a gift. (That alone was worth the interest she'd have to pay on her damn credit cards.)

She opened her sketchbook and quickly, without effort or thought, outlined the view in front her. A quick line for the horizon, another for the hill off to the north shaped like a beached whale. The hillside above the town she sketched in more detail, the terraces, the small farms. Then, for some reason, on the balcony of the tiny restaurant on the point, right where the via della Amore begins, she drew a shadowy group of people. They were sitting in a circle. They had cups in their hands.

§§§

James and Jim B picked Van up as promised. They'd been going to NA meetings for days, hoping to run into the legendary Gato so they could network—and all because James had heard Gato was attending them. Daily. Word was he'd been seen in more than one, per some kind of court order, maybe.

Jim B knew all about court orders.

"It is on the streets," James said, as he pulled into the parking lot of Health Services South, "he has dope from Af-*ghan*-i-stan."

"You sure the dude exists?" Van asked. He was picking at a glob of egg yolk on his tee shirt. Damn. He pulled down the visor. Had he really forgotten to wash his face? He rubbed his hand over the stubble on his chin, then on his head. Rubbed the sleep from his eyes. Oh, well. He guessed he looked the part.

Jim B opened the car door and unfolded himself. His hair hung like a long black snake down his back, making him seem completely vertical. Only his face, up top of the stick of his body, was round. Maybe his nickname should have been lollipop, Van thought, but Jim B it had been since kindergarten. In fact, kindergarten was where Ivan had become Van and Isabel, Zee. Only James had escaped with his name intact.

"War has opened up all kinds of new markets," James repeated for the umpteenth time. He scrunched his spiky blond hair and checked his teeth in the rearview.

"You goin' for the *Less Than Zero* look?" Van asked him.

James ignored him. "Pipeline through Europe. We can get in on the ground floor. I'm telling you."

"Military's bringing it in," Jim B said. "Wanna bet?"

Cool as a cucumber, Van thought. Jim B was his vote for most likely to succeed.

"Whatever." James said. He was tired of selling bundles along with home-burned CDs out of the trunk of his car. He had wanted one thing his whole life: to be a drug dealer. Big time. Figured he could launder the money by investing in the stock market. So what the market was a little iffy now. What wasn't? But who, come to think of it, had ever heard of a *drug* bubble? The war had created his window of opportunity and Gato was the man who could open it.

Once inside the dim room, Van felt like he had entered the limbo of eternal meetings. What circle of hell? He guessed Darlene could tell him. If he remembered to ask her. Another day of stained acoustic tiles on the ceiling, another day of sitting in a circle with a cup of burnt coffee in his hands. Another day of hi, I'm Van and I'm a *fill in the blank*, yes, that's who I am, *all* I am, whatever addiction I've decided to adopt for the day. Heroin-addict-loser, coke-addict-even-sorrier-loser, meth-addict-loser-sorriest-of-all. Defined by substance. By desire. By downfall. By whatever comes before the hyphen. Kind of like being a hyphenated-American, he thought ruefully, defined by something you could not control. Or like being a depressive, a schizophrenic, a suicide. Defined by disease, by flaw, by brain chemistry, by the misfiring of neurons.

So. Today. No different than any other day. He was sitting in a circle of losers: skinny girl in fake leopard skin, Mexican couple, dude looked mean, some kid picking at the scabs on his arms. These people were genuinely pathetic.

"Hi, my name is Jim," Jim B said, "and I'm a junkie."

That, Van knew, was the most he would say for the whole session. He and Jim B used to argue over who got to be the junkie because, as everyone knew, junkies were tortured and mostly silent. Didn't require as much acting as, say, being a coke addict or a sex addict. James liked the flashier roles, of course, but by now, the novelty had worn off. Even for him.

"Can I tell you," Van whispered, looking down at the bitter dregs in his cup, "how much I hate this?"

Hatehatehatehatehate hate this.

James motioned with his head towards the Mexican, squashed nose like a fighter's, all flat against his face.

Van shook his head no. "Name would be Chato, not Gato."

Jim B, with his eyes, laughed.

"Zip-it," James hissed. "Zip. It."

Dude was giving them the evil eye. As was his old lady. She was at least as old as Van's mother. Wrapped in a pink yarn sweater. Probably had pictures of the kids, maybe grandkids, too, in her wallet.

Fuck, Van thought—as if it were an entirely novel insight when, in fact, he had it every time he attended a meeting—this could be my life?

James. How to explain the things Van did for James? The deep shit he got himself into for James. (And Jim B.) Except, of course, that they were the closest things he had to brothers, went back, way back, all the way to Ms. Stuckey's kindergarten, when Van first saved James from the bullies, a pattern that would continue through senior year of high school: James's big mouth and, the only antidotes, Van's quick jokes and Jim B's silence. Jim B, the backup man, because no one could ever figure out what he was thinking, which therefore made him dangerous.

Loyalty had brought Van to this meeting. Loyalty. It was the kind of thing a woman didn't understand, not his mom, not Zee, not even Darlene who claimed that differences between the genders were arbitrarily created by the culture to reinforce patriarchal power structures. (You had to accept that premise, she said, before you could argue that things had changed. Which they had, she said. Thank God. For instance, it is perfectly acceptable in this relationship that I am the smarter and more powerful partner—although weaker physically, which is due, we both know, as much to the fact of my being Asian as female—while you are merely sexy. She pinched his nipples for punctuation. She stuck out her tongue with its round silver stud and waggled it as a promise of more to come. It made him dizzy. She always spoke in complete paragraphs while they had sex because, she claimed, it disconnected his mind from his body and so made his erection last longer.)

Just let me do a little smack, baby, I be hard all night long.

He sometimes said things like that, like he was some old school junkie, because it made her laugh. Mind disconnected from body, weird that words could do that, float into your head, thoughts you weren't even thinking, (sometimes in languages you didn't even understand): *È occupato questo posto?* Or: *epileptic seizures were often mistaken for ecstatic visions.* And you'd think, where the hell did that come from? Some errant radio waves? But sometimes the voice would be as clear as if someone uttered it right next to your ear and so you would zoom into this other reality. For sure it was one reason you did drugs. To leave the here and now. Temporary respite.

Especially when the now included, as it did just now, the Chato-man jumping up from his chair so fast you'd think his balls were on fire.

Crazy *vato* had a knife, Van thought, I could be dead.

Pay attention, the voice in his head said. *Attention, please!* Just like the time the dudes with Uzis burst into the Price Club. *Attention! Cuidado!* Right in his ear and then he felt something or someone push him down so he was lying on the floor next to the stacks of dog food. Who knew you could get intimate with bags of Purina so fast?

But, of course, Gato never materialized. Not at that meeting. And so Van had to confess his sins—*again*—seek absolution from the downfallen, who would not dare cast a stone (unless they were like the current president) because they, too, had got so shit-faced as to do the irrevocable. But what, Van sometimes wondered, what *precisely* was his sin? Being out cold when his dad crashed the car into a telephone pole? The sin, therefore, not so much the drinking of the tequila at his uncle's bachelor's party as the not being conscious, not being able to hold his father in his last moments in life?

Your sin, Zee pointed out, Zee, who brandished truth like a sword, *your sin is that you were* not *sober because, had you been sober, you would have driven and therefore it would* not *have been dad's last moment and your consciousness, or lack thereof, would be a moot point. No?*

Van put his head in his hands. So like Izzy to look not at what *had* happened but at what *could* have happened—to unravel time so that his sin was one of commission rather than omission.

Oh, when would Gato appear? Van felt as if he were waiting for the second coming. Gato as savior.

§§§

It was James's *modus operandi* to light up a blunt as soon as the AC had blown all the hot air out of the car. Roll up the windows. Turn on the stereo. Light up the blunt. That was the ritual, and as Jim B often pointed out, when drug use is ritualized, no *problemo.*

Today, steel guitar, rap, funkadelic influences. Stereo Maracana. Yes.
Liquid guitar with staccato voices. As close to Van's interior music as he'd ever
heard. Smooth, blue undertones, pulsing polka-dots of orange, then red. If he
had his guitar in his hands right now, the sound would go directly from inside
him into his fingers. He just had to find a way to bypass the brain. He just
had to put some reverb on it, reverb up all the way.

By the time they kicked him to the curb, he was inside the music, outside
himself. He had assumed his father's omniscience. He watched himself get out
of the car, check the mail, put the mail back in the mailbox, kick the chain-
link gate open, then closed. He heard them talking about him as he walked
across the yard. They said he looked thin, they liked his new tennis shoes,
they thought he looked like he was waiting for rescue. The voices, they were
not his dad. They were stones dropped into the pool of his own thoughts.
They were subdued today. He put a CD on to drown them out completely, but
beneath the percussion, he could hear them. Chanting. It was ritualistic, as if
some evil were being warded off.

He watched his hands make a sandwich. Sometimes that helped. To focus.
He watched the knife spread the deli mustard, like paint on a brown canvas,
smooth, over every square millimeter of the bread. Five slices of salami. Two
slices of provolone. Cover the salami exactly. Slice the garlic dills lengthwise.
Look how thin he gets them. Look how thin the tomato slices; like paper, the
purple onion. He could work in a deli. He could be a chef. He could turn the
music up a little louder. He could check behind *la velvet Virgen* for a camera,
a two-way mirror. He could go to the store and buy salt. He got in the car.
He hoped the woman was not up on the next street, listening. He hoped
she wasn't a cop. He hoped she wouldn't follow him. He went around three
blocks before driving to the store. He walked into the store and put almost
every carton of salt in his basket. He pretended his shirt wasn't dirty. He kept
his sunglasses on. He didn't look at the person behind him. He didn't look
at the clerk. He watched his finger tap in the secret number. He put the bags
of salt in the trunk. He drove home. He poured it all out, all of it, cartons
of it in a smooth ring along the perimeter of the house. Just inside the fence.
He wanted a circle of white, something that represented light and purity, to
surround them.

Back inside, the house was dark and quiet. He could finally eat his sandwich.
He took a few tokes and filled up a glass with coke. Went online. Last night,

he'd been half-way through mapping a room, a bar, 1940's Germany, with Diego, this dude in Puerto Rico. Van liked practicing his Spanish. Which reminded him. He put on Con Respecto, a cover of the Beastie Boys. Girls. Way Cool. Bumpin'.

Which became knocking, on the front door. When he walked out of the office to answer, there, standing in the living room: his mom. His arm-crossing, toe-tapping, gum-chewing mom. She was wearing scrubs. Even though she was the receptionist, she had to wear scrubs. How dumb was that? She had taken time off from work. She was freaked out because he hadn't returned her calls. Now she was freaked out by the ring of salt around the house.

"What's that all about? Van?"

"Ants," he said.

"Right."

He was trying to keep his head clear but she kept on and on and on, She wanted him to re-check into re-hab—(why all those re's, he had wondered. Re-cidivism. Re-possessed. Was *re* ever good?)—she was worried about him. Why hadn't he re-turned her calls? He needed to be re-sponsible. *Think about somebody else for a change...*

The sound of her voice was making his anxiety spiral out of control, spinning upwards from his chest to his head. Gyro-scope of anxiety, he called it. He tried to picture it slowing down instead of speeding up. Sometimes it worked. But not that afternoon.

"Wait," he told her. "I think I hear Diego. Hear that?"

He went into the computer room, turned down the music. Sure enough, Diego's wife, scolding him in Spanish again. No. There were more than two voices. There was music, a whole Puerto Rican fiesta, complete with laughing children and the whack of the stick on a piñata. But the sound was coming from the computer instead of the headphones. Did he have it on speaker? He checked. No.

"Maybe it's possessed or something."

His mom had a funny look on her face. Ivan, she said. Ivan. Softer. Her hand on his shoulder. Her voice like when they were little. Before his dad died. The old mom. The mom he loved.

"Maybe there's something wrong with the hard drive," he said, pulling the tower out from the wall.

"Level with me. Are you on drugs again?"

"Pot. Only a little pot." He checked the connections. He was going to have to unscrew the back.

"I want you to start going to meetings again."

"Mom. I gotta figure this out. Darlene'll kill me if I messed up her computer."

"Please. You promised Isabel."

"Mom," he said, "Chill. That's all I've been doing. Going to meetings. All frickin' week."

§§§

Darlene came home to a ring of salt around the house and, as far as she knew, a fucked-up hard drive. Van and his bros, James and Jim B, two complete zeroes if she'd ever met one, were sitting on the sofa watching TV and drinking Patrón—it was obscene to pay that much for tequila, she was sorry, especially if you were doing shots—as if there were nothing out of the ordinary about a ring of salt around the house.

Yes, she had saved what was written of her dissertation on the server *and* on her flash drive, but that was not the issue. The issue was that it was her computer and, according to his mother, Van had messed it up. The secondary issue (which was maybe the real issue, although she wouldn't use it because she didn't want to be accused of being emotional) was this: if she complained about the crash of the hard drive or the mess of the living room or even pointed out the weirdness of the salt, *she* would be breaking Van's balls. It was an expression James actually used. According to James, she had Van by the short hairs.

Can we say Dark Ages? Can we say Neanderthal?

They were all three staring at her. Waiting for the explosion.

"Hey, Babe," Van hit mute on the remote, the silence a prelude to apology. "Like I told you, momentary malfunction. Not to worry."

That was an apology? She dropped her backpack on the floor and tried to shake her thick black bangs out of her eyes. He patted the seat next to him on the couch. She sat down, reached for his shot glass and poured some liquid heat down her throat. Why the hell not? She pushed her hair off her sweaty forehead, narrowed her already narrow eyes, and took another shot. She had decided to be, as was often said of the Chinese, inscrutable. (Okay. She was Vietnamese but she could adopt this technique of the ancient enemy of her ancestors if she wanted to.) She could also practice absolute silence. (Silence and feigned deafness, forms of resistance to assimilation practiced by certain tribes of Native Americans, could also be—she knew from her two long years as a graduate student—effective tactics for dealing with those who would colonize you, even if only metaphorically.) Maybe she could make James and Jim B so uncomfortable, they would leave.

Answereth not, she told herself. (And smiled. A private joke. When she and her sister were small, they'd put an "eth" on the end of every verb because it made their speech a code their parents, for whom English was a third language, could never hope to crack. As in, do you loveth me? More than thine bros?) She leaned her head against Van's shoulder and closed her eyes.

"Hey, Babe," he said again.

Still she said nothing. Felt his hand fall heavily on her thigh, his long fingers close to her crotch; the gesture, in front of his friends, proprietary.

She crossed her leg.

He moved his hand.

"How was your class?"

She shrugged. She was waiting.

Van liked feeling the heat of her body next to his even though it was a summer day. Where ever the edge of her body pressed into his, an infusion of calm began to outline him as if with a silver marker, all along his edges, like a shield of light, as if her energy could contain his. He had been jangled all day even though he'd smoked a little *ganja* and indulged in a little tequila to take the edge off. It didn't help that James and Jim B were so amped about finding Gato.

Van looked at the remote in his hand. "You guys want to see the rest of this?"

But James and Jim B shrugged and shook their heads. They seemed to have caught on; they weren't exactly welcome any longer.

"Tomorrow, then," James said. "Ten in the a.m."

"Laters," Jim B said.

Van nodded. He noticed his fingers drumming against his jeans.

Darlene stirred.

James held up his hand in the shape of a phone receiver. Mouthed, call me.

Jim B, echo of James, did the same. "*Pronto, Tonto,*" he said.

As soon as the front door shut, Darlene had one word for Van: "Salt."

He shrugged. "I don't know where I got that idea."

"Your mom seems to think you're trying to keep demons at bay."

"I thought garlic did that."

"Garlic's for vampires."

"I can never keep those things straight."

"Van."

"It must have made sense at the time."

"And my computer?"

"What about it?"

"Your mom said you thought it was possessed."

"Or something," Van stood up and started pacing. "Possessed or *something*. It was a joke. Like I really think a computer could be possessed!"

What was this? An interrogation?

"A *joke*," he repeated. "I've got a substance abuse problem. I'm not crazy."

"Me thinks thou dost protest too much," Darlene said.

He was still trying to piece everything together: there *were* voices in the other room; even his mother had heard them. She had followed him into Darlene's office, after all, and looked at the computer. But her arms had been folded. Those lines between her eyebrows. Had she heard them or not?

"What's up with my mom, anyways?" he asked Darlene. "She called you?"

"Like I was 9-1-1."

He ran his hand back and forth over the stubble of his head, trying to remember.

Darlene laughed. "Your poor mom. I was so annoyed. I told her we'd do some 'shrooms with this shaman I know. To close your negative doors of perception and open the positive."

"I don't know about that." Van shook his head. "Last time I did 'shrooms, I think I saw my own death."

He'd have to ask Zee. (If she'd ever return any of his messages.) She would remember. She had stayed with him. Pretty much all he could remember was her voice. It was soft, a kind of chanting, like today, but only one voice instead of many, a kind of lullaby: Remember how we used to make buckets of mud and we'd pour it down the slide and then we'd slide down? Remember that big old mesquite tree at Nana's? How we'd play camping. And pee in the side yard under the hedge? Or how we'd take chairs and sit and watch the neighbors barbecue through the chain-link fence. Like they were a movie? And then they'd hand us hotdogs and pixie cups of soda?

"Shaman? Van. Now *I'm* joking." Darlene stood up, patted his cheek and kissed him. "I think you need to leave your brain chemistry alone, Babycakes. Even this," she gestured with what was left of a joint from the ashtray, lit it, took a few quick hits and grimaced, "can't be good for you."

§§§

"Mom, are you drinking?"

"Drinking drinking? Or just having a gin and tonic on a hot summer afternoon?"

Zee sighed. It was, what? 3 in Arizona? Maybe 2? A little early for a cocktail. If her mom started now, she'd be sloshed by 8 and there'd be no dinner in between. Unless popcorn scorched in the microwave counted as a meal.

The distance between them crackled with molecules of static electricity and, probably, her mother's irritation. It had been almost a week since the phone call in Riomaggiore. Zee had decided it was a matter of discipline: if she could make herself believe they would survive without her, they would. After all, didn't it demean them to assume she was the one person who could hold everything together? So she'd been turning the phone off. Checking it once a day for messages. But today, of all days, perhaps because it was a Sunday, she had turned it on.

She and Benjy had been almost finished with dinner at Brek Brek and were still lounging at their table outside under the canopy, watching whole families stream by in Piazza Bra, when it rang. She had loaded a plate up at the contorno bar: ensalata mista, roasted eggplant and red pepper and zucchini, fresh tomatoes with basil and mozzarella. He had splurged on trout cooked in a wine and butter sauce. A bowl of pasta with alfredo sauce. A carafe of white wine. They had shared everything, just reaching across the table to take a forkful of whatever they wanted. It was a little scary.

Zee stood up and walked out from under the canopy to see if she could get better reception and a little privacy. People who spoke on cell phones in public always struck her as pretentious and she didn't want to be one of them. She shook her hair so that it covered the hand with the phone.

Her mother's voice came back into focus mid-story: "He put salt all around the house. A circle of salt."

More static. Zee, feeling like an antenna, turned again. A crowd was gathering around a young man and woman who were juggling torches back and forth. His hair was long, in dreds, and his huge baggy pants were held up by red suspenders. She had long shoe-polish-black hair and was oddly beautiful in her bedraggled ballerina costume.

"He kept hearing voices coming from Darlene's computer..."

"Mom. I can't do anything about this."

"He said it had gone haywire. But I couldn't hear anything..."

"Guess what, Mom, I spent four whole days in Florence."

"He sounds, I don't know, like he actually thinks the computer's *possessed*."

Zee couldn't believe this. Her mother knew she had dreamed of seeing the art, especially of Michelangelo, in person since she was a small girl. Since kindergarten, in fact. Zee had known since kindergarten that she loved art—which was one reason she taught art in grade schools. And not just finger painting, no, she taught art history and appreciation. She took huge art books and posters—she had bought plenty on this trip and shipped them back in tubes—with her into the poorest schools in Tucson, where the classrooms were often full of the children of immigrants, where, sometimes, family histories included prison sentences for two or three generations back (for ever how long drug laws had been Draconian, anyways) and those children loved art. They could identify images from the Sistine Chapel. Even the little ones could distinguish between Renaissance and impressionist paintings. Their cubist masks were impressive, and their imitations of Chagall—using the plants and animals of the desert—had hung in several shopping malls. She loved best the brightly colored lizard couples floating in the sky (like the *Bride and Groom*) above fully loaded orange trees or the spires of saguaros or crooked replicas of San Xavier del Bac.

"That's where the salt comes in."

"Now I'm in *Verona*."

"I know, Isabel."

"*Italy*."

"I know. I'm sorry to bother you, baby."

No wonder Michelangelo's unfinished statues in the *Academia* had floored her, she thought, tuning out her mother's prattle, even though roaming on Wind Italia was costing her who knew how much a minute. Okay, maybe it was a *little* dramatic to compare herself to the *Pietá*, but wasn't that the purpose of art? Some kind of universal identification? Catharsis? Mary had brought tears to her eyes, Mary, with her worn face, Mary and Mary Magdalene, struggling to support Him. In fact, all three of them seemed to be struggling together, like the half-finished sculptures of the slaves, to emerge from the stone. That struggle and the rough texture where you could see the marks of the chisel, the effort of its creation, the intention of leaving it unfinished—maybe that was what had filled her with such emotion—the texture itself was evidence of the artist's struggle, wasn't it? Maybe she had felt Michelangelo's love for his creation as well as Mary's sorrow. All that sorrow over the sacrifices they'd *all* made, not just Him. He was God, or the Son of God, after all. He'd *known* what He was getting Himself into.

"Mom. I'm wasting all this money on phone calls when I could be spending it on, oh, I don't know, *dope*."

And then the phone simply went dead.

She turned and saw Benjy staring at her. He seemed amused.

"Okay, that was mean," she said.

"A bit."

"I mean, so *what* Van's pouring salt around the house. I'm in Italy, Mom! Verona! I've met someone. Don't you want to hear anything about my trip?"

"Pouring salt around the house?"

"Not as interesting as it sounds."

They started walking toward the Arena and found—miracle of miracles— a free bench on the Piazza. Near the Sphinx, the huge golden Sphinx for *Aida*—Benjy said Pearl Jam had been brilliant four years earlier—right in front of the white stones of the arena, first century, Roman. Would she ever get over the fact of being there?! She pulled Benjy in front of the Sphinx and kissed him. And then, again, while a Mormon girl on mission from Utah took their picture.

Just then, the phone vibrated. As if on cue: *z call me can u hear them 2*

"I dunno," Benjy said, staring at the message with her. "Seems a bit mad *not* to call him."

She shrugged. "It's probably just our dad."

§§§

There were, at this particular meeting in the middle of a blistering day in the summer of 2004, including Van and James and Jim B and Homer, the fa-cil-i-ta-tor, nine people in the circle: Gato and his old lady, Monica; a young Mexican dude with a nasty scar on his skull; some blonde motorcycle chick; a nerdy white guy who looked nervous as hell. Gato was the man, all right, the main man. Blond hair slicked back *pachuco* style. Van couldn't get over it. Who ever would have thought the bitchassmotherfucker was white?

But maybe he wasn't. There were blond Mexicans, Van knew; just think of the Guzmans, the Hoffmans. Hell, there were lots of blond Mexicans, especially in Mexico. But something made Van think the dude was white. (And since he was half white, he thought maybe that gave him a little authority on the matter.) Maybe Gato had grown up in a Mexican neighborhood, maybe that explained the accent, the gestures, the facial expressions, which were exaggerated, all exaggerated, like *los* crazy *vatos* in the movies. Which, Van suddenly realized, was why he didn't trust him. He had never met a person who actually talked like that. *Suave, que suave ese.* Not since he was a kid, anyways, and his dad had brought around his *pachuco* friends from the old days. His dad? More like his *tata*, man. That was some Original Gangsta shit. Or else Gato was from East L.A. Or else he'd hung out with his *carnales* in the joint for too long. For sure, he'd done time. He was pumped up, tattoos covered both of his forearms. Hell, he had a spider web on his neck. Dude was a walking stereotype.

And what could you say about Monica? She was at least ten years younger than he was, closer to Van's age than Gato's. Slut was the first word that came to his mind though he was trying for Darlene's sake to keep his consciousness out of the gutter. (Style as signifier of *what*, she would ask.) Tight, tight *white* tank. You could see her nipples, they were hard as little rocks. (Style as signifier of sex, he would answer, *availability*.) And her legs, crossed. Bare. Short skirt. One sandal dangling from her toe as she moved the top leg up and down. He didn't even let his eyes go there, to that triangle of darkness that could be one of two things, shadow, or... because he was sure Gato would catch him in the act of trying to figure out if it was her snatch. (Avert your eyes. You don't have to look.) (Right, Darlene.) Blonde hair, dyed, teased, sprayed, fried. Huge hoop earrings. Eyes, dead. Mouth, peachy. Fake fingernails with the white tips, tap-tap-tapping right there on the moving knee and so always bringing his eyes back to the forbidden zone.

Cuidado, eh?

The voice brought Van back into the room. James was playing with his cup. Monica was checking her hair for split ends. Gato was clipping his nails. Everyone, everyone else in the room, the motorcycle mama, the doctor with the prescription drug habit, the Mexican dude with the scar that bisected his head, they were all preoccupied. Especially the stoic and indecipherable Jim B.

Looking in their cups or counting the acoustic tiles on the ceiling.

Eres mío.

Then Van saw why: Homer was homing in.

"Ya'll believe this shit?" he asked him.

Too late. Van had made eye contact. He shrugged. He had no idea what Homer was talking about. "Yeah," he shrugged again. "Why not?"

"Let me tell you why not," Homer said with the sudden zeal of the converted. "I had my jones for twenty years and not once in those twenty years was I ever in a re-la-tion-ship. No, sir. My ladies and me, we always just spoon partners. Pure and simple. Soon as one of us tried to quit, other one was out of there. And so..." he waved his hand dismissively behind him in the direction of Gato and Monica, "you mean to tell me you believe they more than spoon partners? They have a re-la-tion-ship?"

"Yeah," Van shrugged again, holding his shoulders up for a beat longer. "Why not?"

"Based on love and mutual trust?"

Van was stumped. What did Homer want him to do? *Dis* Gato?

"One that can transcend all the negativity of dope and its attendant dysfunctional lifestyle?"

"We don't have to follow the script as it's written," Van said. "We can write our own scripts."

At that, Gato's head came up. He locked eyes with Van's. His eyes were that weird color of blue, *azul turqui*, the murky indigo of eyes that were supposed to be brown but had never turned.

§§§

Zee was stuck. Precipitous is the word that came to mind. Don't look down. This was in the Dolomites. A safe climb, Benjy had told her, even for beginners. Well maintained. But there she was, face sideways against the rough rock—was that pee she smelled? she'd heard people sometimes peed as they were hanging there—right arm stretched as far as it would go, left foot stretched in the opposite direction. She didn't feel like Spiderman so much as splayed, a specimen. She half expected a giant hand to come down, take her left hand, stretch it, pin it to the rock. There she'd be, a dead butterfly.

From below, Benjy shouted sage advice. Her right fingers were going to give, she tested the hold with her right foot and managed to straighten that leg, at least enough so she could reach the next hold with her left hand. This was slow going, although Benjy was right, not so different from the climbing gym where she used to go with Van whenever the lack of drugs in his system made him feel like climbing walls. So they had. Literally. For hours, days on end. She hadn't minded. She was sure she often felt the same as he did, nerve edges rubbed raw, was the way he put it, someone has stripped them of their sheathes. Exhaustion was the only antidote for grief and it was temporary.

A bit further, Benjy called. There was a resting place. Then she could rappel down and sit beneath a tree and draw while he climbed to his heart's content, but she had to make it to that shelf. Her arms ached. She hoped the muscles in her legs wouldn't start shaking. When she pulled herself, with what she thought was the very last bit of her strength, on to the little shelf and turned around—oh, that first moment, so high above everything—she lost her breath, and then she looked at how far she'd come, what was below, the steep wall she'd climbed, the rocky terrain at the base, the trees, the green hills off in the distance, she felt victorious. As if something in her blood had come alive. She felt, yes, it was almost the same as, not the orgasm itself, but the stretching, satisfied, tingly, I-want-to-come-again feeling after the orgasm. She stretched and laughed. Shook out her hands. Looked at her arms and legs, they were young and strong and tan. Her fingers had not let her down. She could do this.

Benjy's spiky red hair popped up over the edge of the shelf.

"You know what I was thinking, d'ye?" His grinning face. His breath coming hard. He pulled himself up next to her and then gave her a big kiss on the cheek. "Maybe your brother isn't a wanker. Maybe he's a bit mad."

"That's news?"

"Clinically, I mean. If heroin quiets the voices, it might be schizophrenia."

Zee didn't know what to say. Van crazy? Didn't everyone hear voices, you know, like other people were lecturing you? Yak yak yak. Definitely voices, but under your control. Still you. On the other hand, her dad's voice felt like his voice, not her remembering his voice. Or imagining what he might say. He still came to her in her dreams, which was different from dreaming about him. And she could *feel* Van. In fact, she had to try very hard *not* to feel what he felt.

Benjy handed her a bottle of water from his pack.

"We see it at Maudsley," he said. "All the time. It has something to do with dopamine. Regular cannabis use tends to amplify the voices—there's nothing wrong with the odd spliff, mind you—but regular use, for some poor souls,

156

seems to bring on psychosis."

Zee started to unpeel a protein bar. Psychosis? Van?

Benjy explained the pharmacology of heroin addiction. The perceived links, although, he said, they could not yet ascertain whether or not there were *causal* relationships between cannabis use, psychosis, and self-medication with opiates. It all had to do with levels of dopamine in the brain. He sounded like the pharmacy student he was. It all whizzed by Zee like so much Latin.

"It's only chemistry, love."

Only chemistry?

"Fuck, you think that's it?" she shook her head. That could be it? Fuck. Only chemistry.

She opened her cell phone: *don't smoke pot.* (she wrote) *it brings voices. home soon.*

§§§

In the car: "Don't let me down, Bro. You're the one he wants to deal with."

(That was James.)

"Maybe if you'd take your eyes off Monica's tits…"

James took his hands off the steering wheel and held them in front of his chest. "She had some nice *melones*. For shore."

"*Muy* sweet," Jim B agreed, lighting the ritual joint.

"She isn't Angelina Jolie," Van said, taking a big hit. "Not public domain."

They were supposed to meet Gato for lunch. Crossroads. Across from the dog track.

"All I'm sayin's, she's his old lady."

"Bad for business," Jim B agreed.

At lunch, James managed to keep his eyes on his tamales, but he went almost immediately into his spiel: had Gato noticed how much harder it was to bring it up from Nogales, say, since 9/11?

Gato smiled. He had evaded even the IRS. He was nothing if not smart. He talked about chopping bikes.

"There's got to be another channel," James said. "Europe's flooded with high grade dope from Afghanistan. Dudes O.D.ing in Norway, for Christ's sake, dropping like flies…"

As if he and Gato were equals, Van thought, CEOs in the corporate world of heroin and high finance when he, James, was really so small time he didn't even have the equivalent of his own hotdog stand.

Gato shifted his eyes towards Van. He didn't comment. Instead, he picked up his fork, concentrated on cutting a bite of his enchilada with the edge of the fork.

"That dude," he said, looking at Van, "that Jesse James, you seen the bike he did for Shaq? Pure art, *verdad*?"

"Smooth," Jim B said. First word he'd uttered.

"There's a dude, here in town, *pues*," Gato was pointing with his fork, "makes Jesse look like an amateur."

All the time, those smoky blue eyes, ignoring James and Jim B, yet measuring Van. James, Gato did not like at all, not his obsequious ways, not the presumed intimacy. James was giving Gato indigestion. Van had seen it happen before.

And Van saw other things, flashes of light, some from high in the window of a building. A body in the back seat of a car. Maybe there were two bodies. The souls faint. It was like watching an old Mexican movie at his nana's when she had only the black-and-white and it flickered every time something exciting happened and so the story was always shadowy and always jerky and always in Spanish. *Eres mío.* He had heard these voices all through group, all through lunch. *Yo te mato.* Or rather, how to explain, he hadn't heard them, exactly, not in his ear. Except for *Cuidado, eh?* The same phrase as before. That was whispered right next to his ear. Definitely external. He could feel the breath of the speaker. Sometimes they were voices, not literally voices, but more like phrases that randomly floated through his brain. As in telepathy. The aural equivalent of an opium dream: sounds you've never heard but that are, nevertheless, vivid and real, as vivid and real as anything in your waking life, a soundtrack of the brain. Whereas *Cuidado, eh?* was uttered. Came from outside. Was, maybe, his dad. After all, the hair had stood up on the back of his neck when Gato asked them to meet him at the Crossroads for lunch. Clearly it had been a mistake to go. Yet he had ignored his gut (even with his father watching over him) and that set him on edge, sent through him a pure rush of adrenaline whenever he considered, objectively, the recklessness of the James and Jim B business venture.

After lunch, when Gato shook Van's hand, he said, "You, I can trust."

And there it was, the foil that held the cure, the only calm in the world, right there in the palm of his hand. Van could see the flame under the spoon, the glass pack syringe, the bodies in the backseat of the car. He could see Darlene, draped across a bed crying, no, revise that—Darlene at a table signing books, her smile insincere, her fame small consolation. He could see a prison cell, then a small room in an old motel where the disabled and discarded rented rooms for three hundred dollars a month. *Te vas a caer*, the voice said. Gato's blue eyes watched. The phone in Van's pocket vibrated. The door of the motel opened and an old man stood there, an old man with gnarled hair and yellowed teeth and nicotine-stained fingers, dirty clothes. He lit a cigarette and waited for his sister.

limbo

I have your son's liver. That's what the woman's voice on the phone had said. Those exact words. "I have your son's liver." And immediately Lena had seen a woman standing, arms outstretched, Rey's liver there, bloody and tender, in her bare hands. She'd felt like swooning, the room tilted. Who was this woman? Why did she have Rey's liver? What kind of witchcraft? Then, just as quickly, another image: a woman in a doctor's smock, the liver floating in a jar of formaldehyde. The room righted itself and Lena understood; the woman meant inside of her. She had Rey's liver inside of her, as in a transplant.

Lena looked out the window. It was early morning. The oranges on the trees were perfectly round and orange, like someone had cut them out of construction paper. There was one white cloud stuck in the aqua sky. The world still looked two-dimensional to her, like a child's drawing, still flat, but at least in color now. For the first year after Rey's death, nothing had had any color. Not that the world had turned black and white, no, not exactly, it had just been dull. Dull and flat. Not worth noticing.

And now this. The woman's voice was grateful. She had small children. Rey's liver had saved her life. She was a mother herself and so she had to thank

Lena for the gift, thought that maybe if Lena knew, it would ease her sorrow. To know her son's life had not been lost in vain.

Lena listened. She had seen shows like this on television, where the recipient met the grieving family. Maybe that's what the woman wanted, to go on *Oprah* or something. She sounded like she'd been reading a script: every day I thank God for your son's selfless act. It was what they all said. And then the family of the dead person cried and said what a healing, comforting thing it was to know that their loss had been someone else's gain.

Lena could just see herself on one of those shows—they wouldn't *want* to hear what she'd have to say. She'd never been one to lie, not even to herself, so how could she be philosophical about Rey's death? Rey hadn't wanted to die. No higher good had been served. He was twenty-two years old. Murdered. Blamed for his own murder. He had died for nothing and some woman getting his liver was not going to change that.

When she finally found her voice, she was very calm. She said, "Don't ever. Call here. Again." And then she quietly hung up the phone.

"How could this have happened?" Lena asked her husband.

Over a year later, to get this phone call? Impossible. Impossible that this woman had his liver. He had died on the street. 2 a.m. Bled to death. It had been cold. He had been alone. And then the yellow police ribbon for how long? Hours? Hours before the phone call from the hospital?

"Don't you have to sign papers?" she asked him. "I didn't sign any papers. You didn't sign any papers."

"No," Rafael shook his head. He didn't understand it either. "Maybe it's just one of those things. Where they know what hospital or town and so they go through the obituaries. Find someone who died young on that same day. Of an accident."

He put his heavy hand on Lena's shoulder and gave it a squeeze. He knew to keep his voice matter-of-fact and his touch minimal but reassuring. Otherwise, she might collapse, give in to her sorrow again. There had been days when all she could do was lie in a dark room and, when he'd get home from work and he tried to gather her up, it was like trying to hold someone made of jelly. Parts of her kept melting away, out of his arms.

Maybe it would've been different, he thought, if they'd had other children. Or if Rey had had a child, but as it was, grief was all she had left. And he understood that. Still, sometimes he was so tired. Sometimes he didn't know how much longer he could bear to be the backbone for both of them.

"Both him and Eddie were in the paper together," he said, puzzling through the evidence. "Did Olivia get a phone call asking about Eddie?"

Lena shook her head yes.

"From the same woman? Saying she had his liver?"

Yes again.

"See?" He kissed the top of her head and then retired with his beer into the living room. "That's all it is, then. Some nut. Just guessing."

She sighed. So. Rafael was right. That was all it was. She had signed no papers, he had signed no papers. And besides, didn't they have to do it right away? Within minutes of death? Isn't that why they kept the person on life support? She wanted to ask Rafael this, he would know. He watched those medical programs on TV; even the operations, he watched. And he had the kind of mind that could remember everything. But she knew he didn't want to talk about it any more. He held his grief inside him, in a small place, like a tumor. It wasn't safe for him to let it out. Hers, she knew hers was cancer already; it had spread throughout her body and was eating everything. She would never recover.

She lay next to him on the sofa, put her head in his lap. She needed to feel the roughness of his jeans against her cheek, the reassurance of his flesh inside them. She'd always liked the way he smelled, even in his work clothes, like laundry left in the sun. He was watching boxing. He was the only one now, the only one she really loved. If God took him, the house would be too empty to bear.

He and Rey had filled it, especially in the late afternoons, when they'd come home from work, all dusty, and Rey would tell her about the idiots on the job. One time, he'd thrust his arms in the air above him, like he was the electrician on the ladder, and then jangled all over to show how the jolts had gone through him when he touched the live wires. Shit, Rey had laughed, the dude would've *fried* if dad hadn't kicked the ladder out from under him.

Rey was always joking like that. Any situation, he could see the humor in it. At family parties, he was a magician, even from when he was little, doing card tricks no one could figure out. Not his aunts and uncles, not even Rafael. Everyone loved his sudden laughter, the way his dark eyes flashed right before he pulled a coin out of his little cousin's ear. He'd always thought he could fix anything by making Lena laugh. Or by amazing her. Once when his nana was sick, he had tried to make her little dog disappear. Lena could remember her mother, how she could barely sit up, she was so weak, and there was Rey, fourteen, and he'd run out of card tricks. He made a little stage out of a box in his nana's bedroom and, abracadabra, Paco was supposed to disappear down into a trap door but, instead, he started playing tug of war with the towel Rey was using to whisk him into invisibility. Rey kept his composure. He turned his back and then, when he turned back around, flourishing his cards like a fan, there was a wiggling lump under his tee shirt. Lena remembered her mother laughing, laughing so hard tears were streaming down her face. That was one of her last memories of her mother. And now Rey was gone and she knew what a broken heart was. Not just broken. Ripped out. Ripped from life, that's what the priest had said, as with the claws of the lion.

She closed her eyes and concentrated on Rafael's hand as he smoothed her hair away from her face. Its weight, its warmth. The scratchy calluses. She sighed. So. The woman had just been guessing. Reynauldo had gone to his maker whole. Which was as it should be. Sure, they had passed his clothes down, his stereo and CD's, even his precious truck. Nothing had been wasted, everyone had something to remember him, but a liver was not a pair of shoes. God intended no passing of internal organs from one person to the next. Of this, she was certain. You had to be whole on Resurrection Day. Maybe it didn't make any sense. She knew the body decayed in the ground and if God could fix that, surely a few missing organs wouldn't make much difference but, still, this was her son. She wasn't taking any chances. Scripture was scripture.

Besides, it was macabre. Harvesting. Even the word *harvesting*, when applied to a human body, was ghoulish. They would have to cut into the body. It would not yet be cold. If someone touched the hands, it would feel like the person was merely sleeping. Maybe there would still be the flush of life under the skin, breath in the lungs; maybe you would feel like the person was still inside, could hear you when you said goodbye. Said you loved him. It would happen in that moment she had never had with Rey. She had been robbed even of that.

She opened her eyes in a panic, grabbed Rafael's hand and pressed it to her mouth. She wanted to cry. The body would still be warm and that bothered her. Had they lied to her? Taken Rey's body to the hospital before he died? And how would they know when it was hopeless? How could they be sure? When they reached in, to take the heart, for instance, was it still beating? Was it warm when they held it in their hands? And then, then—she could see this so clearly—then they placed it like it was a slab of meat into a little ice chest marked "Playmate" and put it on an airplane headed for some other body. In some other state. An empty body. In need of a heart.

"Shhh," Rafael said, as he pulled her up to him. "Shh."

He could hear the accelerating panic of her thoughts, feel the release of acid inside her.

Whenever Lena imagines the night of Rey's death, she imagines it as a story. It's the only way she can bear to think about it at all. Plus, she hadn't been there and the only reliable witnesses are dead and so she, like Rafael, has pieced that night together as if it were a mystery. Sometimes she sees it in a series of scenes, almost like an episode of *Homicide*. The images are skewed, they flash quickly, and just like on *Homicide*, when you get closer to the truth or to the moment of revelation, you see the same shot several times, but all jerky, and from different angles.

First the camera pans the apartment complex, the nearly deserted parking lot, the Mexican couple being questioned off to one side, the late model Chevy, one door open. The camera zooms in, focuses on Eddie, slumped behind the wheel of the car, the windshield shattered by the fatal bullet. Then on Rey, lying half in and half out of the car, as if he were trying to get in so they could speed away. Rey still has the shotgun in his hands. The white detective nudges at his body with the toe of his shoe. He shakes his head, sure it was a shoot out. The Mexican detective, younger, continues to circle the car.

Jump cut: close up on the security guard as he's being questioned by the two detectives. He's a white guy, looks a little like a cowboy, since this is Tucson. First night on the job, so he's jumpy. He points to a small hill in front of the car, then over toward the buildings. "I came out of that courtyard there and I see these two guys standing here, on the grass. They're arguing with that man and that woman." He points to the couple being questioned by another cop, over under a tree. "I can hear by their voices that there's going to be trouble. Then I see one has a shotgun, so I yell something, like, hey, what's going on here? They all turn and look at me and then these two guys start backing up towards their car. Fucking lights're coming on, that's all I need, buncha gangbangers poppin' off outta the windows, and so I yell at them to put the gun down and that's when I hear the shots. I swear to God, they just start fuckin' shooting. They're almost to the car and I'm up here with no cover. But I musta hit 'em 'cause it gets real quiet. And then I hear the sirens already and you guys are here before I can even call it in."

The white cop looks at the Mexican cop and shrugs. They walk off a few feet and Smythe whispers, "The dude *is* a cowboy, fuckin' rent-a-cop redneck, but the rest of it pretty much jives with the physical evidence."

They walk back over to the car and circle it. The guy in the driver's seat is a mess, face all cut up from the flying glass, bullet must have hit the jugular, blood everywhere. The other guy, the shooter, hit in the upper torso. Small entry wound, seems to have bled out. Maybe it hit the heart or some major artery. Hard to tell.

"Little weird the windows aren't broken, given the way he's lying…" The Mexican cop points this out to his partner.

"Prob'ly got hit over there," Smythe gestures towards the grass.

"Had to be one strong mo'fo, to get from there to here, with a bullet in his chest."

"I've seen people run blocks. They wanna live bad enough."

Moreno shakes his head. It's a possibility, he supposes. They walk back to the rent-a-cop and tell him they see no reason to hold him. "But stick around," they've already confiscated his gun, "the County Attorney's office will be in touch."

The cowboy swaggers over to a crowd of people who have gathered near the curb. Lights a cigarette. Begins bragging about how he took both of them out.

"Thought he was afraid of all the gangsters and the wannabes…"

"You know how it is, Manny, he's gotta tell his war stories."

But Moreno is looking over at the couple under the tree. Some Mexican Mafia dude with his hair in a ponytail. Original Gangster, for sure.

"May as well have a sign on his forehead."

"You think?" Smythe laughs.

And the woman is witchy, hair so lacquered it would crackle if you touched it. Has to be his old lady. Skanky dope fiend, jittery as hell.

"Drug deal for sure," Moreno says. "Or someone owed someone something."

"Yeah," Smythe snorts, "coupla gangbangers we don't gotta worry about no more."

Moreno gives his partner a look. "I ever tell you how much you inspire me?" he asks. He feels a twinge of anger, but not at Smythe so much. Everyone knows he can be an asshole. No, he feels it for the two dead kids, their parents, their whole huge families that do nothing to keep them out of trouble. Fucking Mexicans, he knows that's what Smythe's thinking, and so

Moreno tells him what his dad used to say, "There are Mexicans and then there are *Mex*-icans. Just like, there are blacks and then there are niggers." Same inflection.

Smythe doesn't seem to get it.

"All people have their low-lifes. That rent-a-cop trailer-trash your cousin, for instance?"

Smythe laughs. "That's what I like about you. Your unique point of view."

"Probably felt like this was his lucky day, one get-outta-jail-free chance to take out a coupla brown people."

"Shit, Manny, the kid had a gun."

"*Shot*gun." *That* is what bothers Moreno about the whole thing. Not so much the intact window, but the fact that the kid had a twelve-gauge, choked for a wide spray, like he was hunting birds. Not to kill. Not a human being. It wasn't sawed off or nothing. And if he'd had any intention of shooting the cowboy, or anyone within yards of him for that matter, they'd be peppered with those pellets. "How the hell did he miss?"

"Just a dumb kid. There are bigger mysteries in the world than that."

Moreno sighs. Poor kid probably thought flashing a shotgun was protection enough. Must've shot it up in the air, a kind of warning: *We're bad.* Didn't know you had to be ready to kill. "I'm gonna go check out Old School," he tells Smythe, and they both amble over to the conversation beneath the tree.

Old School is short and cocky, his black tee shirt stretched tight over a chest made muscular by years of pumping iron, arms thick and covered with prison-blue tattoos. Turns out he's fresh out of the joint. He's done his time, paid his debt. No parole, no tail, as he puts it, a free man. Free to hang out with felons and known users, free to frequent wherever the hell he wants. He's not holding. No weapon. Angelique—gang tattoos of her own, red nails curved like talons—is his ex. And she happens to live here, with his kids, he says. He's just visiting. Has a right to see his kids, you know. He sticks his chest out for punctuation. "Hey, man, me and my old lady, we're the *victims* here. They were trying to jack us."

He repeats this several times but jack them of what, no one can tell, since neither one of them has any money on them, nor is his car in that part of the lot. The more the dude shoots off his mouth, the clearer it becomes, at least to Moreno, that Angelique—with her raccoon eyes and two-toned lipstick all bitten off—is just a little afraid of her ex; that the driver Eddie—they now know his name and that he was married, two small children—had been her lover, until recently, when he went back to his wife; and that Old School, before he got sent up—and probably again now, no reason to believe he's changed professions—was an enforcer for the Mexican Mafia. Someone who collects debts for a living.

"Still, what do we do with the cowboy?" Smythe asks as he and Moreno fill out their report. "Things may have worked out the way Old School wanted..." he points out, "but..."

Moreno finishes it: "that doesn't mean he's guilty."

In Lena's mind, the camera pulls out, pans the whole scene until it rests on the car. The two victims are shown, click-click-click, three freeze frames, as the camera jerks back, in black and white, from a greater and greater distance—as if the only things that matter now are the answers to Moreno's questions.

At the hospital that night, Lena had collapsed. Rafael had identified his son's body, had held Lena so she could be tranquilized, and then had taken her home and put her to bed. To keep himself from falling apart, he decided to drive by the crime scene. By the time he got there, the night was already fading to dawn. It was an eerie scene. In the tawny light of almost morning, the yellow police ribbons were more incandescent than any sun or moon or street lamp. He steeled himself, decided it was his duty as a father, his last duty, to find the truth and, to do this, he knew he would have to be as cold and practical as a scientist, ready to accept anything as long as it could be verified by evidence.

The car was still in place. Detectives were standing around, comparing evidence. Rafael noted the shattered windshield, driver's seat soaked with Eddie's blood, noted that the gunfire came from the direction of a small hill, just the other side of the sidewalk, where cops were milling around looking at the ground. He walked over to the passenger side, noted the still-open door and the ground stained with Rey's blood. He had a moment where he lost his balance, felt sick, but then he remembered Lena's wail in the hospital, how it had escaped when she saw the bluish tint of Rey's skin. That had sent her over the edge, that, and the scratches on his face from flying glass. She had touched his face and this ungodly animal *no* had pierced Rafael, cauterized the wound in his heart, closed something down inside him. Tamped down the grief. None of this was real, he couldn't let it be real.

He made himself take a breath, look over to the west. The desert was still there; oddly enough, the world had not changed, not visibly. The desert was still green, and beyond it the Tucson Mountains were still black and toothy. He and Rey had often gone hunting there. That was where he would imagine him, still walking through those mountains. Not here, not dying, not alone, not cold in the morgue, but there, still walking. There, over by Baboquivari, with the spirits of the Indians. Rafael took another breath and, by force of will, made his mind clear and hard. He had to see this through.

The first thing he noticed was the intact window on the open passenger's door. Neither was the windshield in front of Rey broken. Impossible that he had been shot from the same direction as Eddie. There were bullet holes, downward trajectory, in the front seat of the car, in the roof of the car. He looked up to his right. Whoever shot Rey had been standing in the window of one of those apartments. There had to be at least two shooters.

Detective Moreno walked over and asked Rafael if he needed help. Even though he thought he should keep tabs on Rafael, he didn't take him seriously at first. Maybe it was because Rafael reminded him of some farmer, some easygoing, heavyset Mexican dude, his fingers as thick as sausages. Maybe because he talked slow and deliberate as water.

But Rafael had Moreno pegged immediately. He recognized in him the same serious demeanor of the doctor who'd showed them Rey's body. It was the demeanor not of true sympathy or empathy but of: what a shame, what a shame your son has done this, what a shame you did nothing to prevent it. A kind of distancing, necessary, Rafael supposed, in their lines of work, but a distance none the same. A distance that said he and his son did not belong to the same category of humanity. They were the fallen, the ones who had brought this upon themselves, who deserved whatever had happened.

Rafael knew he would never be able to trust this Moreno, so it was no surprise when Moreno gave him not what he himself had deduced, but what the cops must have all agreed upon as the *official* story: Moreno explained that Rey had opened fire on the security guard and that the guard, who was standing on the small hill, returned fire, killing Eddie as he sat in the driver's seat and, possibly wounding Rey before he could open the car door.

"We speculate," Moreno said, "that your son's wound was so severe he died before he could get in the car."

Rafael just jerked his head back in what he hoped would suffice for a nod of agreement, but inside, his heart pounded at the lie. He didn't trust himself to speak. He knew they would close the case as quickly as possible. Who was

Rey to them? Just another dead Mexican. After all, it had been open season on Mexicans and Indians in Arizona for a long time, and that the cop's name happened to be Moreno this time, well, that didn't seem to make much difference. Rafael knew he had perhaps only minutes to record everything he could see. Every trace, every bit of evidence. He needed to remember it all, down to the smallest of details.

"So what're you looking for over there on the grass?" he finally asked.

"Just procedure. To thoroughly comb the scene."

"No buckshot over there, huh?" He wanted Moreno to know that *he* knew what was up.

No, Moreno admitted, they hadn't found any. Yet.

Rafael scratched his head. "I'm no mathematician, well, but I'm a hunter, and so it seems to me that if Rey had been aiming *at* the guard, he would've hit him, at least some scratches." He paused.

Moreno didn't respond.

"*¿Es la verdad, no?*"

But Moreno didn't respond in Spanish which would've indicated, at least, some small link between them.

"And there would be buckshot over there on the ground where they're looking," Raphael continued. "Now, if he'd been aiming higher, say over the guard's head, the arc would be higher and longer and you'd be wanting to look out farther, say over in the lot behind that little hill." He paused again. "Plus, the spent casings would be over there, near the curb, whereas, they're here, to my right."

"Hmm," Moreno said, "good point."

"Actually, didn't you say my son started shooting first, on his way to the car? Wouldn't there be casings in a trail, in that case?"

This had occurred to Moreno, too. Things weren't adding up the way he'd thought they should, and if the father was right, if the shooting didn't break out until the driver was in the car and the shooter almost in, then the guard was lying. At least about the sequence of events, about when the shots first rang out. But why would he lie about that? Confusion? Maybe.

"They were obviously almost able to get away. Why start shooting at that point?" Rafael asked.

"Don't know." Moreno shrugged. "Maybe they thought it was safe to start shooting then. Like a drive-by. Happens all the time." He made his eyes flat and emotionless. It was his poker face, his detective mask, so useful when dealing with the parents of dead children.

"Only cowards do drive-bys," Rafael said. "My son was not a coward."

"Maybe the guard wasn't the one they wanted dead."

"Or maybe someone wanted *them* dead," Rafael bit off his words. "If he'd wanted to shoot someone, he wouldn't have missed, not from that range, not with a shotgun." He looked up at the apartments again. "Whoever killed my son," he pointed to the windows, "shot from up there. You know it and I know it. The guard may have shot Eddie, but the bullet that killed Rey came from there."

"We've interviewed the residents…"

"The only question is why." Rafael pointed first to the bullet holes in the roof of the car and then indicated, again, with his hand, the line to the middle window. "If you check up there, I bet you'll find your scatter pattern. It'll be faint, but if Rey shot anywhere, that's where he aimed." And then he pointed to the casings on the ground.

Moreno nodded. It was the only thing that made sense. Problem was, they'd already interviewed everyone. They had no suspects. In fact, technically, the *suspects* were dead. Technically, everybody else was either a witness or a victim.

Rafael was waiting for Moreno to speak, to say what they both knew was true.

He leaned against the car, put his hand on the hood, and was suddenly filled with Rey's presence. It was strong, tangible, like being filled with heat, like a flash of heat and light. Blinded, Rafael could see everything, could see through Rey's eyes, could see darkness, see him, Eddie, running next to him, backward, towards the car, some security guard yelling at them to stop, telling him to drop the shotgun, there's the glint of light on metal as the guard pulls his gun out and waves it at them. Rey cocks the shot gun, but he doesn't shoot, he's just getting it ready in case he has to. Eddie's yelling at him to get in the car and, out of the corner of his eye, he sees Eddie's in, he's trying to get the key in the ignition, and so Rey pulls his door open. Just then, shots ring out and there's a spray of bullets, but from over his head. He turns toward the apartment building, the bullets are raining down from up there, a figure in the window. He fires up over the trees, aiming in that general direction, but higher than the windows. Back off, he's thinking, back off, mother fucker. Then, just as suddenly, shots from his left. The fucking guard is shooting at them and in that instant, as he turns his head to the left to see the guard and he fires toward the building again, there's the crack and shattering of glass and he knows Eddie is hit, and then there is the punch in his chest, it knocks the wind out of him, a searing pain, and he is falling with the force of it, trying to hide behind the door, bullets and glass spraying all around. He can't hear Eddie, there is a burning in his chest and he can't breathe, and neither can Rafael, seeing all this.

Rafael's chest was tight, he found himself stumbling toward the apartment building, which he now saw in the daylight, all blurred and wavy, as if through summer heat. Rafael touched his chest. He didn't know if this clenching of his heart was grief or a heart attack, but he brought himself out of it, thinking, you can't have a heart attack now, Mom would kill me. *Mom.* It was Rey's voice in his head, Rey's sick humor, and Rafael knew what he'd just seen was the truth.

Rafael was exhausted. His insides felt like they'd been scrambled, liquified, and so to open the door of his house and see all the family there felt like walking from one unreal world into another. The house was full of his wife's sisters doing what women do even in times like this, making food, quietly gossiping, wiping the noses of small children, scolding the older ones. He figured that was why women were like the force of nature, they kept things going. Even in time of war, they would be scavenging crusts of bread, dipping them in water and holding them to the mouths of babies. Like last summer— the drought in Mexico had been going on for years, nothing was growing, there was nothing to eat—and the women held up a train, a train full of dried corn they would take and grind to make tortillas. Remembering those women made him want to weep, partly because they were heroic but partly because their story made his own troubles seem small. Yes, he had just lost his only son, yes, his world had been shattered and this pain was like nothing he had ever felt before, but they had lost children, *children* lost for lack of water and food when just miles to the north, there was plenty. It was as senseless as what had happened to Rey.

Lena was sitting in the old rocker. She had Eddie's youngest, Maricela, not even six-months, pressed to her chest. Like a tourniquet, Rafael thought, apply pressure to the wound. Lena looked at him and forced a grim smile. Her eyes were pleading, make this go away, I can't bear this, and he knew, at that moment, she would've traded all the children in Mexico for Rey. All the children everywhere. She just wanted her son. She just wanted the one thing he would never be able to give her. He had to look away. He had always been the man who provided whatever she needed and now he could do nothing. That was gone. Who they were was gone.

Eddie's wife Olivia was lying on the couch with their little girl, Daniella, cradled in her arms. They were both asleep, face to face, their dark hair curling wildly against their plump cheeks. Both were just children, Rafael thought, babies, too young for such sorrow. Olivia's face was slack, they must have given her something like they'd given Lena. The girls, he and Lena had always thought of them as their grandchildren. Rey had been their *nino*, not only because he and Eddie had been friends from childhood, but because he and Olivia were like brother and sister. Once Lena had insisted that Rey was in love with Olivia, but Rafael had refused to listen. He didn't want to know the nooks and crannies of other people's hearts, not even his son's. It was like those *novellas* his mother used to watch on TV, people torturing themselves with what they couldn't have when life could be simple and good.

Lena motioned for him to sit next to her. "That *bruja*," she whispered hoarsely, "that Angelique, she called Olivia three times last night. She called and said, 'Eddie is going to die tonight,' and then she hung up."

He sat down. Took his baseball cap off and ran his hand through his thinning hair. "She wanted to kill him because he left her?"

Lena shrugged. "Her husband just got out of the joint. Maybe *he* wanted to kill Eddie." She patted Mari on the back. "He was one of those, you know, *familia* guys. Mexican Mafia. Who knows how those people think."

Rafael moaned and leaned his head back on the headrest of his chair. Moreno hadn't told him nothing about this but suddenly it all made sense. He dug the heels of his hands into his eyes until the sky rockets behind his lids matched those going off in his gut. This was why his son had died? Because of some lovers' triangle? Because some people didn't know what was true and lasting and because others mistook revenge, petty revenge, for honor?

Olivia, lying on the couch, was half in and half out of sleep or stupor or grief, she didn't know exactly what it was. There was pain and then the not-pain of disbelief. There was the stab in the heart and then the heavy, wet cottony feeling, choking her, fogging her head. It couldn't be true. When she'd heard the yap of the screen door, she'd expected to hear Eddie's voice, or Rey's. Not Rafael. But Eddie. Eddie telling her: bad joke, Babe.

Why had she listened to them last night? Why had she believed in them?

Why hadn't she called Rafael the first time she got the call? He would have gone to the Branding Iron. He would've stopped it right there. Everything would be different.

But, no. When the first call came, Eddie and Rey had been playing pool, and so she had shrugged it off as Angelique being the bitch she was. Plus Olivia knew her old man was just out of the joint, so she figured Angelique had to put on a show, prove she didn't want Eddie any more.

Olivia knew the truth. And she knew Angelique knew. Eddie was the one who didn't want *her* any more. He had made up his mind. There was a change in him. He wanted a life with Olivia and the girls. It was as if he were overcoming a terrible addiction; he was a little shaky, true, a little hung over, but his will was strong. His eyes were open. She could tell he wanted her again. And he wasn't coming back out of duty. No, there was desire and love again, in his eyes, in his voice, in the way he touched her at night.

She half believed what her mother had told her: Angelique had bewitched him, but the magic had run its course. Now, whatever he had felt for Angelique, he would feel double for her. She was forgiving. With her, he could be his best self.

The second phone call had made her uneasy. Angelique's voice was a growl, rough with anger or jealousy. She said his name *Eddie* as if it were a curse. As if she were cursing him. "Eddie is going to die tonight."

Olivia called over at the Branding Iron, but the bartender said they'd already left. Just as she hung up the phone, they walked in. They had both been drinking, but they weren't drunk. Eddie was full of bravado but Rey, Rey was quiet. Bad sign. Rey not joking. She could tell they were both shaken. Evidently, Angelique had gone into the bar with her ex-husband, his name was Mario, and a few of his buddies. They had started some shit and the bartender had told them all to take it outside.

"Mario was wearing one of those long black *pachuco* coats," Eddie laughed.

"Dude thinks he's some badass O.G. from East L.A. or something." Rey rolled his eyes at her, but when Eddie went to take a piss, he told her it was scary there in the parking lot. It had been dark, like maybe they'd broken the streetlights out before they'd gone into the bar, Rey didn't know, but it was dark dark. Way darker than usual. They all went out and stood off toward the back, Eddie and Mario, facing off. The other guys were there, in a circle, ready to jump in. Ready to take him out if he jumped in to back Eddie up. Rey was sure Mario had a gun, in his waistband, somewhere hidden underneath that coat. He started bumping up against Eddie telling him things like, what, Eddie thought it was cool to bang his old lady while he was in the joint? How would he like someone to bang *his* wife? Maybe it could be arranged. He'd heard she was sweet. Payback was a bitch. What goes around comes around. He'd heard she was *real* sweet. Young. Not skanky like old Angelique over there. He'd looked at his friends and they'd laughed.

"As you do unto others so will they do unto you," Mario had said, "twofold." And he bumped up against Eddie again. "Maybe threefold. Or four." He bumped him again, like he wanted Eddie to start something so he could take him out, call it self-defense.

Rey said he remembered looking over at Angelique. She was just standing there, tapping her foot, her arms crossed in front of her breasts. She looked more bored than pissed. "I almost expected her to start filing her nails," Rey laughed.

The cops had come right after that and made them break it up. They'd told Rey and Eddie to go on home and had kept Mario and the others in the parking lot.

Olivia remembered how Eddie and Rey had sat around the kitchen table drinking beers, then shots, talking about the whole damn thing. She'd told them they should call the cops, file a restraining order, or something, because of the phone calls, but they said, what good's that gonna do? It's not illegal to call people. Threats aren't illegal. The cops'll just say there's nothing they can do until a crime has been committed.

"Fuck," Rey had laughed, "half the time they don't arrest people *after* they do something. They're sure as hell not gonna arrest 'em *before* they do something." He shook his head. "Filing a complaint, exact wrong thing to do."

"Just make you look like you got no balls," Eddie agreed.

"These guys, they want you dead, you *will* be dead."

"Olivia, me and Rey, we gotta fucking watch our backs all the time."

"It could happen anywhere. Any time."

"In a parking lot, in a mall, in front of the house, in front of the girls. Shit. You can't dick around with guys like Mario. You got to show 'em what's up."

"They think you're scared, it's over. They see you're not, they leave you alone."

"No shit."

"You gotta take care of business."

This was how they went on, their whole line of reasoning, and Olivia knew it was true. You couldn't live like that. Always wondering. Better to take fate in your own hands. Fucking confront the guy. Be in control.

She sat there and listened and the more they drank, the faster and louder they got, like a monsoon which, once begun, gathered its own momentum, its own destructive force, and there was nothing she could do about it.

Besides, she was half convinced they were right. Better to go tonight. Find this Mario alone, without his crew. And she knew they had to take a gun. Rey was right. Mario would have one. There was no getting around that.

If she hadn't known better, she would've thought Eddie was doing coke again, he was so on edge. He pulled her onto his lap and nuzzled her neck. "No one is going to hurt my *chula*," he promised.

She looked across the table at Rey. He was as quiet as Eddie was jumpy. Rey was serious. "Let's do it," he said.

Even though Rey was a few years younger than her and Eddie, he had always been their protector. When Eddie was in school and the other kids used to taunt him, Rey was the one who clowned around until they quit. Or else stood up to them. For years, he'd been taller than Eddie, but it wasn't just his size. There was something *in* him the other kids respected and tonight, even though he'd recently bleached his hair out and tattooed a comet on his shoulder, even though he looked like Dennis Rodman or one of those weird singers on MTV, she still believed he could keep Eddie safe. It had always worked before. He had even, once, come in between Eddie and his stepfather. And *no* one was meaner than his stepdad on a drunk.

They rose from the table, they put on their jackets. Rey got the shotgun from the closet, the shells from the top of the cabinet in the kitchen. Eddie called over at Angelique's and when Mario answered, he said, "Be in the parking lot. South side of the building." Then he hung up and looked at Rey. "Let's fucking do it."

Olivia watched from the window as they climbed in the car. She stood there for a long time, it seemed, remembering how it felt when Eddie kissed her, feeling Rey's hand on her shoulder, watching to see if any cars with their lights out were coming down the street. It was so still her heart hurt. She wasn't sure, now, that they were going to do the right thing.

The plan was that Mario would come down to the parking lot. That's why they'd called. They didn't want to go up to the apartment. Too dangerous. Besides, they didn't want to scare Angelique's kids.

"Bad enough they've got her for a mother," Rey had said.

Olivia went into the girls' bedroom and gathered them up into her arms and carried them, first the baby, then Dani, into her and Eddie's bedroom at the back of the house. Just in case. As soon as she got Dani in bed, the phone rang. The sound sent a jolt through her even before she heard Angelique's voice. And this time, the voice was so matter of fact: "Eddie is going to die tonight." As if it were simply true. And there was nothing anyone could do to stop it.

Sometimes Lena imagined she called the people who wrote *Homicide* and told them the whole story. They could have made an episode about it, shown the truth. Those cops would have seen that things weren't as they seemed. They would have asked more questions, arrested Mario and Angelique, figured out the connection between them and the rent-a-cop, found the other shooter, and charged them all. They were all guilty. Rey and Eddie were dead because of all of them. The black detective, Pembleton, the one with the bald head and the fire of righteousness, he would have seen through their stories. He would have proved they were guilty in the eyes of the law as well as in the eyes of God, but then he was a Catholic and he valued the truth. To him there was such a thing as justice.

But, no, that was not how it happened. They didn't have a black cop who was determined to find the truth. Instead, they had a white cop who was happy to cross Rey and Eddie off his list as gangbangers or drug dealers, who made it clear that this would've happened sooner or later anyway, and who figured their deaths made his workload more manageable. And a Mexican cop, Moreno, she hates the term Tío Taco but it does come to mind, who felt that every Mexican kid who went wrong was some kind of personal reflection on him, and so to save himself embarrassment, he was as much of a dick to Rafael as the rest of them.

Instead, the investigators from the County Attorney's office were no better than useless. They interviewed the same people the cops had interviewed and declared the security guard blameless. A victim. Not only that, but Mario and Angelique were victims.

Rafael had been furious. What about the bullet holes in the roof of the car? the scatter pattern above the windows in the apartment building? the spent shotgun casings right next to the car? the angle of Rey's entry and exit wounds? the fact that there were 22 spent shells where the security guard had been standing? The guy had to *reload*. Or someone standing next to him had been shooting, too. What about that, he had wanted to yell at Moreno. What about all the physical evidence? The over-whelming physical evidence?

These questions became his litany. He ran through them over and over at work. He couldn't sleep at night. He began to haunt the apartment building, looking for clues, asking questions of everyone he met. Then one day he bumped into a thug in the parking lot. The guy held his hand up like it was a gun. "It was that easy," he said.

Rafael exploded. Everything in him that had been tamped down, all the grief, all the rage, suddenly flared up from his gut into his head. He found himself lunging towards Mario. He would throttle him, if it was the last thing he ever did, he would throttle him. He wanted to crush Mario's throat in his hands. And then he heard the cry. He looked down. Mario was grasping his little daughter by the wrist and she was looking up at Rafael. Terrified.

Mario laughed. "And it would be that easy, again, old man."

After that, Rafael decided to hire a private investigator. They would sell the house if they had to, but they would get the cops to do something about Mario. At least they could do that.

"It's worse than I thought," the PI told Rafael and Lena. "Just for instance. You already know that there were only three shotgun casings. Your son shot three times. Yet in the police report, the security guard said Rey fired *six* times. Plus, the entry wound came from above." He paused to let that all sink in. "Okay, the guy in the third-story apartment was an Air Force guy, owned a gun of the same caliber that killed your son but, since the cops determined he was not a suspect, no evidence was gathered. Since no evidence was gathered, he can't be considered a suspect."

A Catch-22 if Rafael had ever heard of one.

"Could be this Mario hired him. After all, he knew Eddie and your son were coming and went down to the parking lot to meet them. Or, could be this guy figured he was protecting his family. He was of that mindset, you know, here I am in the military, serving my country and this is the best I can afford. Section 8 housing with all the 'scum of the earth.' His words exactly." He shook his head at Rafael. "Either way, whatever the motive, the shot that killed your son came from one of those windows. But you already knew that. The thing we will never know is *who* pulled the trigger, or *why*."

"Security guard see shots coming from up there?"

"Not according to the records. But I can't interview him. Not him. Not Mario, not Angelique," the PI shook his head. "I can't even contact them. They're all considered *victims*, not witnesses. Courtesy of the Victim Protection Act. My hands are tied."

"So there's nothing we can do to find out?" Lena had asked.

The PI shook his head, "Hell, the Air Force transferred the guy. He's outta here."

"No way Mario would go out to meet them *without* a gun. Unless he had backup." Lena pleaded.

"I know it. You know it," the PI said. "*They* know it."

"So we can't clear his name? We can't even clear his name?"

Rafael knew hopeless when he saw it, but he still promised her: "We can try to get them to reopen the case."

Rafael would never describe to her how it felt to sit in that small white room, across the table from Moreno and Smythe. He watched as Smythe fluttered the papers in the folder the PI handed to him. Did he read any of it? No. He simply turned to Rafael and explained patiently, as if he were an idiot, or a Mexican who didn't understand English, that his son was a criminal: he had a high blood alcohol level; he was the one who had gone to the victim's place of residence; he was the one with the shotgun. The police officers had broken up the altercation at the bar, let him go home. He should have just stayed home.

"But, instead, his actions directly precipitated,"—do you understand pre-cip-i-tated? this was Smythe—"your son's actions directly precipitated the violence that evening."

And then Moreno. "He went, with his friend, to threaten the friend's ex-girlfriend and her husband. The guard was shooting in self-defense. The shots fired from the window, if there *were* any shots fired from the window, were fired in self-defense."

Was Moreno apologetic? He was unable to meet Rafael's eyes. He stood up.

What would you do, Smythe wanted to know, if someone was shooting at the apartment where your family was sleeping?

"Your son, we know this is hard for you to accept, your son was the suspect here. Not the victim. Your son was the criminal. I can't say it any more clearly than that."

Lena had listened to her nana's and then her mother's stories long enough to know that the lives of the dead got reduced to a few sentences. "Your great-grandmother was a very tall woman. When the gold rush came and the Americans drove them off their land, she helped drive the horses and cattle all the way from their ranch in California, all the way across the desert and mountains, here to Tucson. She was just a small girl." That was the life of Ramona Ronquillo Sereno as it had been passed down to her. Sure, for a while, there must have been whole stories, maybe how she loved horses so much she'd slept in the barn with them or maybe how she had fallen in love with the boy on the neighboring ranch when they were both babies in the crib, but with each generation, the stories had become more and more distilled until now, all that was left of her was two sentences, two characteristics, really: height and horsemanship. And then, finally, because Lena could not pass so little down and because she had no one to pass it down to, even those two sentences would stop. With her, Ramona Ronquillo Sereno would disappear altogether as if she had never existed.

With Rey, too, there had been whole stories; they had come unbidden, one upon the other in that first wave of grief. It was almost as if the stories themselves could stave off the finality of death: no, here, the image of him so vivid, the details so precise, how could such a thing be possible? How could he no longer be *real?* This was her disbelief. She'd reach her hands out in the air, how could he *not* exist when his physical body had been so solid, so full of life? Even from when he was a baby, he'd had more life in him than his body could contain. And now it was gone? So quickly? So suddenly? A rent, a hole in the universe. She'd felt like she could part the fabric of it, become invisible, enter eternity, and find him. Hear his smart-ass remarks, his sudden laughter. Feel him, hold him once more, smell him. But, like his smell on his shirts, he was fading. Could matter be so ephemeral? Could a body disappear like that?

His flame, in the cave of souls, had been extinguished by mistake, she was sure of it, but there was nothing anyone could do. And now, it was the end of new memories. The stories were already becoming more succinct; she noticed this when she sat around and drank coffee with her sisters. Every day, some of the details would drop off, some were forgotten, others changed, and others, because remembered, heightened. The memories were becoming like a series of snapshots, frozen in time, isolated until he came to be defined by them. Lena hated it. His death, so traumatic that, for others, it had become the most memorable part of his life.

She, Lena, his mother, remembered *him*, her living son. The way his eyes had fastened on her when she nursed him, his little legs so chubby she hadn't been able to fasten the plastic pants over his diapers, his headlong run as he learned to walk. Or, how he had hated school, always, hiding behind a tree, even when he was only seven. He had loved basketball, skate boarding, anything physical. Music. Girls. Tequila. Magic. Life was an altered state to him, he lived it so intensely.

Rafael had said as much at the funeral: Rey had lived each moment so fully, it was as if he had lived *two* lifetimes in twenty-two years. Somehow that thought had comforted Rafael, but nothing comforted Lena. She had wanted Rey to have everything. Everything. And it had all been taken away from him. He would never get to finish his life.

His life had been reduced, this was what she hated most, his life had been reduced to one sentence: that he'd been killed in a shootout, that a security guard had killed him in self-defense. Rey's life reduced to a *lie*. The security guard had not killed him. Friendship had killed him. His love for Eddie had killed him. For Olivia. For the girls. Loyalty, love, youth, misjudgment. A desire to protect. An unwillingness to kill another. Those were the things that had killed him.

In the end, Lena knew nothing could be done about the liver—they would never find out the truth just as they had never found out the truth about his death. That night, lying next to Rafael, hearing his breathing turn heavy, she couldn't help but think about it. Oh, she could have gone to the hospital, she supposed, and like in one of those TV shows on the Lifetime channel, snuck into a dark room full of file drawers. By luck or cleverness, she would open just the right drawer and there would be Rey's file. Evidence. Proof of what they had done to him.

But she knew this was just another fantasy. They would never record their own sins, not in any language. No, when she thought of the police or of the doctors, she got the same picture in her mind: a large white building, all the shades are drawn, inside there are long, narrow corridors, signs pointing every which way, secret rooms where terrible things happen. It was a foreign place where she would never be able to understand them. And it wasn't that the police and the doctors spoke only one language, no, it was that the language they spoke came directly from the mind, it never passed through any other major organ.

This was why they could make such a surgical separation, body from soul.

Reynauldo in life, worth nothing to them, expendable. Not even worthy of justice. And yet his body, in death, so precious, that they wanted to waste nothing; each organ they wanted to rob and pass on to another.

That night in her dream, she saw legions of pregnant Mexican women wrapped in *rebozos*, waiting at the border, being allowed to come across to give birth. It was a bad science-fiction movie: their children would be fed, inoculated, allowed to grow—but for one reason. So their organs could be harvested. In her dream, Rafael said, what? That surprises you? Lena had shrugged in response. When she was a girl, her nana had told her that white people were like vampires. It had scared her but, with some of her teachers, it had seemed like it might be true.

Then the phone rang. And when she answered it, it was Rey. "Mom," he said, "don't think like that. Things have changed." Then he started telling her what he'd done that day, ordinary things, how he'd seen Olivia and the girls at the park. "Smell that?" he said.

She did. It was roses.

"I can pull them out of the air now. Any color you want."

But all she wanted was him. She listened to his voice. He didn't realize he was dead. There was so much she wanted to ask him. How was he? Was he sad? Did he miss his life? But she couldn't ask him those things because then he would know he was dead and then he would never call again and she would never hear his voice again. She had to be very careful and just listen.

"Well," he said, "gotta go."

"Reynauldo," she said. "Wait. Please."

Then she woke up. She felt even emptier than usual. She rolled over and put her hand on Rafael's chest. He was awake. He had been crying. She had never seen him cry. Even through all of this, he had never cried.

"Did you hear Rey's voice?" she asked him.

"You know, I never thought of karma this way," he whispered. "I always thought it was one on one. You know, you steal and down the line, someone steals from you. But I never thought of it as cumulative. That because of all the things I did when we were young, drinking, staying out late with the guys, I guess they all added up... I just never thought it would catch up with me in this way."

"Rafael," she said. "Oh, Rafael. We don't deserve this."

"We didn't teach him to value his own life."

And then, like the woman in the Bible who loved too much, Lena felt herself turn to salt. She was rigid. She was going to shatter. She felt him touch her arm, rub her arm and then, with both hands, her back, over and over. He was sobbing. His skin was rough, his hands heavy as birds, their wings battering her cold flesh.

She couldn't respond.

He thought it was grief.

"Shh," he whispered, his voice hoarse, "shhh. We have to let him go."

But she couldn't. Not even for Rafael did she want to live in this world.

Publication Acknowledgments

"Just Family" appeared in *Ploughshares.* Vol. 31, Nos. 2&3, Fall 2005.

"Emily's Exit" appeared in *spork* 2.2, Spring/Summer 2003.

Beth Alvarado

photo by Barbara Cully

A graduate of the Stanford and University of Arizona writing programs, Beth Alvarado has published stories in *Ploughshares, spork, Northwest Review,* and *Calyx,* among other publications. *Not a Matter of Love,* her first collection, won the 2005 New Rivers Press MVP (Many Voices Project) Competition. She lives in Tucson, Arizona, where she teaches at the University of Arizona.